The notation was in her father's h
of any emergency call Perry Masc
no one else."

Muriell made no effort to check the swinging door this time as she dashed from the dining room into the kitchen, out of the door from the screened porch, across a strip of lawn to the door which opened into her father's workshop.

She flung open the door, called, "Daddy!".

Stepping inside, she came to a sudden halt.

A chair had been overturned and broken. A sinister red pool had spread out over the cement floor.

The floor, spotted here and there with fine sawdust, was literally covered with currency. The bills were all in a denomination of one hundred dollars . . .

Erle Stanley Gardner (1889–1970)

Born in Malden, Massachusetts, Erle Stanley Gardner left school in 1909 and attended Valparaiso University School of Law in Indiana for just one month before he was suspended for focusing more on his hobby of boxing than his academic studies. Soon after, he settled in California, where he taught himself the law and passed the state bar exam in 1911. The practise of law never held much interest for him, however, apart from as it pertained to trial strategy, and in his spare time he began to write for the pulp magazines that gave Dashiell Hammett and Raymond Chandler their start. Not long after the publication of his first novel, *The Case of the Velvet Claws*, featuring Perry Mason, he gave up his legal practice to write full time. He had one daughter, Grace, with his first wife, Natalie, from whom he later separated. In 1968 Gardner married his long-term secretary, Agnes Jean Bethell, whom he professed to be the real 'Della Street', Perry Mason's sole (although unacknowledged) love interest. He was one of the most successful authors of all time and at the time of his death, in Temecula, California in 1970, is said to have had 135 million copies of his books in print in America alone.

By Erle Stanley Gardner
(select bibliography)

Perry Mason series
The Case of the Sulky Girl (1933)
The Case of the Baited Hook (1940)
The Case of the Borrowed Brunette (1946)
The Case of the Lonely Heiress (1948)
The Case of the Negligent Nymph (1950)
The Case of the Moth-Eaten Mink (1952)
The Case of the Glamorous Ghost (1955)
The Case of the Terrified Typist (1956)
The Case of the Gilded Lily (1956)
The Case of the Lucky Loser (1957)
The Case of the Long-Legged Models (1958)
The Case of the Deadly Toy (1959)
The Case of the Singing Skirt (1959)
The Case of the Duplicate Daughter (1960)
The Case of the Blonde Bonanza (1962)

Cool and Lam series
The Bigger They Come (1939)
Turn on the Heat (1940)
Gold Comes in Bricks (1940)
Spill the Jackpot (1941)
Double or Quits (1941)
Owls Don't Blink (1942)
Bats Fly at Dusk (1942)
Cats Prowl at Night (1943)
Crows Can't Count (1946)
Fools Die on Friday (1947)
Bedrooms Have Windows (1949)
Some Women Won't Wait (1953)

Beware the Curves (1956)
You Can Die Laughing (1957)
Some Slips Don't Show (1957)
The Count of Nine (1958)
Pass the Gravy (1959)
Kept Women Can't Quit (1960)
Bachelors Get Lonely (1961)
Shills Can't Cash Chips (1961)
Try Anything Once (1962)
Fish or Cut Bait (1963)
Up For Grabs (1964)
Cut Thin to Win (1965)
Widows Wear Weeds (1966)
Traps Need Fresh Bait (1967)
All Grass Isn't Green (1970)

Doug Selby D.A. series
The D.A. Calls it Murder (1937)
The D.A. Holds a Candle (1938)
The D.A. Draws a Circle (1939)
The D.A. Goes to Trial (1940)
The D.A. Cooks a Goose (1942)
The D.A. Calls a Turn (1944)
The D.A. Takes a Chance (1946)
The D.A. Breaks an Egg (1949)

Terry Clane series
Murder Up My Sleeve (1937)
The Case of the Backward Mule (1946)

Gramp Wiggins series
The Case of the Turning Tide (1941)
The Case of the Smoking Chimney (1943)
Two Clues (two novellas) (1947)

The Case of the Duplicate Daughter

Erle Stanley Gardner

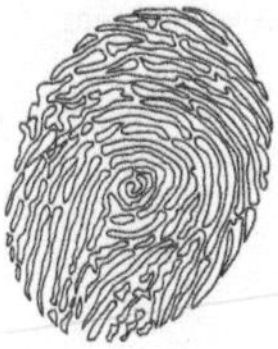

An Orion Paperback

This edition published in 2021 by
The Orion Publishing Group Ltd
Carmelite House
50 Victoria Embankment
London EC4Y 0DZ

An Hachette UK Company

10 9 8 7 6 5 4 3 2 1

A CIP catalogue record for this book is available from the British Library.

ISBN (mmp): 978 1 4719 2087 5
ISBN (ebook): 978 1 4719 0873 6

Printed and bound in Great Britain by Clays Ltd, Elcograf S.p.A.

FSC www.fsc.org
MIX
Paper from responsible sources
FSC® C104740

www.orionbooks.co.uk

FOREWORD

The field of legal medicine is exacting, and it is a difficult field in which to achieve distinction. Relatively few men have gone to the top of the ladder.

The good medico-legal expert knows more about detective work than Sherlock Holmes, as much or more law than the average lawyer, and must be firmly grounded in all branches of medicine. In addition, he must have a quick, perceptive mind, be able to express his thoughts clearly and concisely and have such self-control that he can't be rattled or enraged by the sneering type of cross-examination with which some attorneys try to embarrass a medical witness.

To achieve international distinction in this field is an honor indeed, and it is a distinction that has been achieved by my friend, Doctor Francis Edward Camps.

Dr. Camps is as much at home working with Scotland Yard on some puzzling matter as he is rendering services as a consultant while visiting friends in the United States. There is no room here to list his honors in England, but in the United States he is a member of the Harvard Associates in Police Science, and a Fellow in the American Academy of Forensic Sciences. He has written a most interesting book dealing with his work in the famous Christie case in Great Britain (*Medical and Scientific Investigations in the Christie Case*—Medical Publications

Ltd.) and that book alone shows the outstanding qualities of the man: his painstaking attention to detail, his innate shrewdness, his thorough training and, in addition to that, his ability to express himself so interestingly that this work, which is really a scientific treatise in post-mortem detection, reads as absorbingly as any mystery novel ever written.

In addition to this, he has recently, in collaboration with Sir Bentley Purchase, written a book on forensic medicine entitled *Practical Forensic Medicine,* a book which is destined to become a leader in the field.

Dr. Camps has visited at my ranch, and has shown himself to be a warm, human, personable individual. He can relax in the company of his friends and be so genially casual that one has a hard time associating such a warm and informal personality with the medical genius who has followed seemingly insignificant clues to bring murderers to death, criminals to justice and, on occasion, exonerate persons wrongly accused of crime.

In dedicating this book to Dr. Camps I am keenly aware that he wouldn't want to be singled out as an individual, or given any personal publicity. He is, however, keenly interested in improving the public understanding of legal medicine and so I feel sure that he will accept this dedication as a part of my effort to make the reading public familiar with the importance of legal medicine to their daily lives, to their human rights, and to their safety.

Altogether too many murders have been diagnosed as suicides and, unfortunately, too many suicides have been held to be murder. It is difficult for the public to realize the hairline distinctions which must be made by a competent examiner.

Because the medical examiner is inherently modest, the public knows all too little about the extent to which its safety is protected by this group of men who have dedicated their lives in a most difficult field. A good expert in the field of legal medicine must first learn enough medicine to qualify himself as a medical doctor, then acquire enough experience to reach the highest income brackets if he chooses simply to practice medicine. Then he must study enough law to qualify as an expert. (In fact, many of these men do take the bar examinations and become attorneys at law.) Then he must specialize in pathology, go on to study crime detection, learn all there is to know about poisons and poisoners, and then deliberately obscure himself in the relatively low-paid field of forensic medicine so that he can be free to do good in the world in his chosen calling.

The public owes this unselfish and devoted body of men a great debt of gratitude.

And so I dedicate this book to a man who has achieved international recognition in a most difficult field—

My friend,
FRANCIS EDWARD CAMPS, M.D.

ERLE STANLEY GARDNER

CHAPTER ONE

MURIELL GILMAN, moving from the dining room into the kitchen, was careful to hold the swinging door so it wouldn't make a noise and disturb her stepmother, Nancy Gilman, who usually slept until noon, or Nancy's daughter, Glamis, whose hours were highly irregular.

Muriell's father, Carter Gilman, was hungry this morning and had asked for another egg and a slab of the home-made venison sausage. The request was unusual and Muriell felt certain the order would be countermanded if she gave her father an opportunity to reconsider, so she had hesitated over actually starting to warm up the frying pan. But after it appeared her father not only definitely wanted the added food but was growing impatient at the delay, she eased through the swinging door, leaving her father frowning at the morning paper, and turned on the top right-hand burner of the electric range.

Muriell understood her father very well indeed, and smiled to herself as she recalled his recent attempt to lose weight. This added breakfast order was probably open rebellion over his low-calorie dinner of the night before.

They lived in a huge, old-fashioned, three-story house which had been modernized somewhat after the death of Muriell's mother. Muriell had been born in this house, knew its every nook and corner and loved it.

There were times when she felt a qualm at the idea of Nancy occupying her mother's bedroom, but that was when Nancy wasn't physically present. There was something about Nancy, a verve, an originality, a somewhat different way of looking at things, that made her distinctive and colorful. One could never resent Nancy Gilman in the flesh.

The sausage, which had been frozen, took a little longer to cook than she had anticipated. Having delayed starting to cook it until her father had shown signs of impatience, she had then put the egg in a frying pan that was a little too hot. As soon as she saw the white begin to bubble she lifted the pan from the stove. The egg sputtered for a moment in the hot grease, then subsided.

Muriell's father liked his eggs easy over and very definitely didn't like a hard crust on the bottom or at the edges.

Muriell turned the stove down and cautiously returned the frying pan to the burner. She tilted the pan, basted the yolk with hot grease so as to expedite the cooking process and then skillfully turned the egg over for a few seconds before removing it from the frying pan.

Arranging the egg and the sausage on a clean plate, she gently applied her toe to the swinging door between the kitchen and dining room and gave the door a shove, catching it on the rebound with her elbow so that the jar of the return swing would be minimized.

"Well, here you are, Dad," she said. "You—"

She broke off as she saw the empty chair, the newspaper on the floor, the filled coffee cup, the smoke spiraling upward from the cigarette balanced on the side of the ashtray.

Muriell picked up her father's empty plate, slid the new plate with the egg and sausage into place, put a piece of toast in the electric toaster and depressed the control.

As she stood there waiting for her father to return, her eye caught an ad in the paper, an ad which offered unmistakable bargains in ready-to-wear; so Nancy stooped, picked up the paper and became engrossed in garments and prices.

When the hot toast popped up in the electric toaster, she became frowningly aware that her father hadn't returned.

She tiptoed to the door of the downstairs bathroom, saw the door was open, and looked inside. No one was there.

She moved around the downstairs rooms, then she called softly, "Daddy, your food is getting cold."

She returned to the dining room, then, suddenly alarmed, she made a complete search of the downstairs part of the house.

Could it be possible that her father had gone to work without so much as putting his head in the kitchen . . . ? He knew that Muriell was cooking another egg and sausage. He had specifically asked her to do this. He certainly wouldn't have left the house without an explanation. Even if there had been some sudden emergency at the office he would have let her know. But there hadn't been any emergency at the office because the telephone hadn't rung. There was an extension in the kitchen and Muriell would certainly have heard the bell if there had been a phone call.

Something must have happened which caused her father to go upstairs, then. Could it be that Nancy had been taken ill?

Muriell hurried up the stairs, trying to be silent but so intent upon speed that her feet made noise, and when she tried the knob of the bedroom she was in a little too much of a hurry and the latch gave a distinct click.

Nancy Gilman wakened, looked at Muriell standing tense in the doorway and said, "Well, what is it?"

"Father," Muriell said.

Nancy glanced over at the empty twin bed with the bedclothes thrown back. "He left an hour ago," she said irritably. And then, suddenly catching herself, smiled and said, "What's the matter, child? Is he late for breakfast again?"

"No, it's all right," Muriell said. "I put on another egg for him and . . . well, I wanted to tell him it was getting cold."

For a moment there was just a flicker of annoyance on Nancy Gilman's face, then she raised herself to one elbow, punched a second pillow into submission, piled it on the first, smiled at Muriell and said, "You're *so* considerate." And then, after a distinct interval, added, "Of your father, my dear."

Her smile was enigmatic. She dropped her head back to the pillow and closed her eyes.

There was no other place her father could possibly be unless he had gone to the attic.

A sudden disquieting thought entered Muriell's mind. Recently her father had been rather upset. He had told her only two nights before, "Muriell, if you should ever be confronted with any emergency in connection with my affairs, remember that I *don't* want the police. Do you understand? I *don't* want the police."

Muriell had looked at him in surprise and had tried to question him as to what he meant, but his answers after that were smilingly evasive. All he had wanted to impress upon her was that he didn't want the police and he had managed to impress that upon her very thoroughly.

So Muriell, with a vision of sudden suicides, of bodies hanging by the neck from the rafters, literally flew up the stairs to the attic.

The big place was filled with the usual assortment of old boxes, trunks, an old dress form and a couple of antiquated rocking chairs. There was a smell about the place, the aroma of unpainted wood, that warm atmosphere of quiet, secluded detachment from the rest of the house which is somehow the property of old attics.

On the lower floors of the house life could go on with the constantly increasing tempo of modern civilization. But up here in the attic, removed from the rest of the house, occupied with the insignia of bygone days, there was an atmosphere of calm tranquillity as though the rapid pace of modern civilization had slowed serenely to a halt.

Something about the attic reassured Muriell. She walked around under the eaves just to make certain that no one was up there. By the time she descended the stairs she was in a much calmer frame of mind.

At the foot of the attic stairs she encountered her stepsister, Glamis Barlow, fairly bristling with indignation.

It was entirely in keeping with the character of Glamis that her sleeping garments would be of a clinging, almost transparent material, the upper garment extending only a few inches below the hips, the lower garment so brief as to be all but invisible. Her honey-blond hair framed blazing blue eyes.

"*What* in the world are you doing prowling around the attic at this time of the night?"

"Oh, I'm sorry, Glamis," Muriell said. "I . . . I was looking . . ."

"Well?" Glamis asked as Muriell hesitated.

"I had to go up there for something," Muriell said. "I tried to be quiet."

"You sounded like a team of horses up there. You were right over my room."

"I'm sorry."

Abruptly Glamis laughed and said, "Forgive me, Muriell. I'm a beast at this time in the morning. Is there coffee downstairs?"

Muriell nodded.

"I'm terrible until I've had my coffee," she said. "I'll come down and have a cup and then go back and go to sleep. You're all finished up in the attic?"

"Yes," Muriell said. "Don't bother, Glamis. I'll bring you a cup. You want it black?"

Glamis nodded.

"I'm sorry I wakened you. I was getting breakfast for Dad."

"In the attic?" Glamis laughed.

Muriell gave her a gentle pat. "Go get back into bed, honey, and I'll bring you up some coffee."

"It's all right, honey," Glamis said, "but Hartley Elliott is spending the night here and I know he needs his sleep."

"He is!" Muriell exclaimed.

"Yes, dear. He's in the Rose Room. We got in at a terrible hour this morning and came up to sit for a while on the porch. When he tried to start his car it seems he'd left the ignition on and the battery was run down.

"So I told him he could spend the night."

"Does Nancy know?" Muriell asked.

"Of course not, silly! Nancy was asleep. Did you expect me to waken her to tell her I'd invited a house guest? I'm twenty, you know, and if you're thinking of the proprieties—"

Abruptly Glamis broke off, then a smile bent the corners of her mouth. "Aren't I the old savage bearcat in the morning?"

Muriell patted her again. "I'll bring you coffee, honey. Get under the covers. You're all but nude."

"I am, aren't I?" Glamis said, smoothing her palms over the sheer gossamer of her garments. Then she laughed, and her bare feet moved silently down the carpeted corridor.

Muriell went downstairs, convinced now that for some reason her father must have gone to the office without coming out to say good-by. He must have thought of something that he had neglected to do; perhaps some important appointment that he had forgotten about.

Muriell was quite cheerful as she poured coffee from the electric percolator and put a couple of pieces of thin dry toast on the tray for Glamis to nibble on. Glamis was a creature of curves and she wanted to keep those curves at their seductive best. In the evening she'd overlook a calorie or two but in the morning her breakfast consisted of very thin, very crisp toast and black coffee.

Glamis was snuggled up in bed and duly grateful. "Oh,

you dear," she said. "You thought to bring some toast!"

"Hungry?" Muriell asked.

"Starved," she said. "I always wake up with a tremendous appetite. If I let myself go I could really go to town on breakfast."

She propped herself up in bed, ground out her cigarette in the ashtray, reached for the coffee cup, looked at Muriell, said, "I don't know how you do it, Muriell."

"Do what?"

"Keep that bodily machine of yours functioning so smoothly. You're just radiating calm, competent energy. I'm a clod until after I get my coffee, then it takes me half an hour to get human."

She broke off a piece of toast, bit into it and sipped the coffee.

Abruptly she pushed the rest of the toast and the coffee cup away from her on the table, smiled at Muriell and dropped her head on the pillow. "Thanks, darling," she said. "I'm good for a couple of hours now."

Muriell left the room, closing the door gently, went back down to the dining room. It was the cook's day off but the maid who came in by the hour would be in later and clean up the dishes.

Once more a feeling of uneasiness possessed Muriell as she looked at the dining-room table, the one egg on the plate, the sausage, the newspaper on the floor. It was so unlike her father to leave without saying good-by, so unlike him to be inconsiderate even in little things, and he knew that Muriell was out in the kitchen. . . .

And then she saw his brief case.

Under no circumstances would her father have left for the office without his brief case. She knew that he had some papers in it he had been working on the night before and he expected to do some dictation on those papers the first thing at his office. He had even taken the cardboard jacket containing the agreements out of the brief case at the breakfast table long enough to verify some point, and had made a notation.

Muriell crossed the room, picked it up and opened it.

The agreements, stapled in their legal-looking blue covers, were in the brief case.

Muriell pulled them out, looked at them and then saw a notation on the cardboard jacket in which the agreements had been placed.

The notation was in her father's handwriting. It read: "In case of any emergency call Perry Mason, the attorney, at once. Call no one else."

The memo had her father's initials on it and was written in ink. There was a slight smear on the last initial, as though the filing jacket had been hurriedly replaced in the brief case before the ink had had an opportunity to dry. There was also a telephone number, presumably that of Perry Mason's office.

Could this have been what her father had been writing at the breakfast table?

Muriell looked at her watch. It was ten minutes before nine. She replaced the brief case, went back to the dining room and then, approaching the table, suddenly realized that her father's napkin wasn't on either the chair or the table. Her quick search revealed that it was nowhere in sight. Wherever her father had gone, he had taken his napkin with him.

Suddenly the significance of that missing napkin impressed itself on Muriell's mind and once more aroused all of her fears. She looked under the newspaper, under the table, through the dining room, even out to the reception hall near the front door and then up the carpeted stairs toward the second floor. It was then she thought of the workshop.

Of course!

Back of the house was a huge, long, single-story building which contained three garages on the north end. Then to the south of the last garage there was a darkroom where Nancy did her developing and enlarging and, immediately to the south of the darkroom, the last room in the building was a workshop where Carter Gilman indulged in his twin hobbies—working with modeling clay and making wooden objects, inlaid cigarette cases of rare woods, jewel cases, sewing boxes and various ornamental gadgets.

Muriell made no effort to check the swinging door this time as she dashed from the dining room into the kitchen, then out the back door of the kitchen to the screened porch, out of the door from the screened porch, across a strip of lawn to the door which opened into her father's workshop.

She flung open the door, called, "Daddy!"

Stepping inside, she came to a sudden halt.

A chair had been overturned and broken. A sinister red pool had spread out over the cement floor.

The floor, spotted here and there with fine sawdust, was literally covered with currency. The bills were all in a denomination of one hundred dollars and to Muriell's startled eyes there seemed to be hundreds of them.

On the other side of the room, to her right, was a door

which opened into Nancy's darkroom. In front of this door on the cement floor was her father's missing napkin.

Muriell stepped over the napkin, pushed open the door of the darkroom.

The acrid smell of fixing bath assailed her nostrils. Light, coming from the open door, served only to intensify the shadows at the far end of the room.

"Daddy!" Muriell called.

Silence engulfed her voice.

Muriell crossed the darkroom to fling open the door which led to the garages.

The sports car and the club coupé were there in their proper places, but the sedan was missing.

Muriell, her heart still thumping, considered the problem of the missing sedan. Her father must have left the dining-room table, gone to the garage still carrying his napkin. Some sudden emergency had taken him out there before he realized the napkin was in his hand.

He must have gone to the garage first, from the garage through the door to the darkroom, then crossed the darkroom and opened the door to the workshop.

What he had seen in the workshop had caused him to drop the napkin.

Then what had happened? What was the significance of the overturned, broken chair? What was the significance of the money spread all over the floor, and above all, that spreading red pool?

Muriell, reaching a sudden decision, hurried to the telephone on the counter of Carter Gilman's woodworking shop, depressed the button which gave her an outside line and called her father's office. When she learned her father was not there, she hurriedly leafed through the phone book on the counter and dialed the number of Perry Mason's office.

The voice that answered the telephone assured her that Mr. Mason was not in but that his secretary was there.

"I'll talk with his secretary," Muriell said.

A moment later a reassuringly competent voice said, "This is Della Street, Mr. Mason's confidential secretary."

Muriel poured words into the telephone. "I suppose I'm completely crazy," she said, "but my father has disappeared. I found a note in his brief case to call Mr. Mason in the event of any unexpected development and . . . well, there's just something mysterious about the whole thing. I—"

"May I ask your father's name, please?"

"Carter Gilman. My mother is dead. I'm living here with him and my stepmother and her daughter. We—"

"Your name, please?"

"Muriell Gilman."

"Can you give me your telephone number?"

Muriell gave it to her.

"And the address?"

"6231 Vauxman Avenue."

"Mr. Mason just came in," Della Street said. "I'll call you back within five minutes."

"Thank you," Muriell said, and hung up.

CHAPTER TWO

Perry Mason, walking over to his office desk, grinned at Della Street, eyed the pile of mail on his desk with distaste, said, "Who is that you are promising to call back, Della?"

"A Muriell Gilman. Her father is Carter Gilman. I wanted to check the card index of clients, but I don't think we have anything on him."

Mason frowned a moment thoughtfully, then said, "There was a Gilman on one of my juries not too long ago. I've forgotten the first name. What's it all about, Della?"

"His daughter thinks he's disappeared."

"Gilman . . . Gilman . . . Carter Gilman. That name sounds familiar. Look him up in the jury cards, Della. I think he was one of the jurors in that case where it turned out there had been a mistaken identification."

Della Street moved over to the card index. Her nimble fingers ran through the cards of Mason's confidential file of jurors and said, "Yes, here he is. Carter Gilman. He was a juror on that Jones case. You have him marked as exceptional. It's the same address, 6231 Vauxman Avenue. Now wait a minute. Vauxman Avenue—*that* rings a bell."

Della Street turned from the file, opened the appointment book, said, "A man who gave his name as Edward

Carter telephoned yesterday and asked for an appointment sometime today. I gave him an eleven-thirty appointment. I asked him for the address and he said he was visiting here in the city with friends on Vauxman Avenue. Let me look up the number. Yes, here it is, 6231—the same address."

"And this man gave the name of Edward Carter?"

She nodded.

"And Muriell says her father's name is Carter Gilman?"

"That's right."

"Did this Edward Carter say what he wanted to see me about?"

"Said it would be a consultation on a very confidential, personal matter and he'd like to have at least half an hour."

"And he has the appointment?"

"That's right, at eleven thirty. I gave him the appointment. You'll find it on your appointment card."

"And what about the daughter?"

"I told her I'd call her back. She seemed terribly upset. I don't suppose there's anything anyone can tell her."

"Get her on the phone," Mason said. "I'll talk with her."

Della Street dialed the number, said, "Miss Muriel Gilman, please. Just a moment, Miss Gilman. Mr. Mason will talk with you personally."

Mason picked up the phone, said, "Mr. Mason, Miss Gilman. Now what was it about your father?"

"I feel terribly silly," Muriel said, "but my father was eating breakfast. I stepped out in the kitchen to refill his plate. I'd cooked fried eggs and homemade venison sausage. He'd asked for a second helping. He sometimes eats a very hearty breakfast and then seldom eats any lunch. When I came back with the sausage and egg he was gone."

"Nowhere in the house?" Mason asked.

"I couldn't find him anywhere."

"How many eggs had he eaten?" Mason asked.

"Two, and two big slabs of sausage."

"Let me ask you," Mason said, "whether Carter is his first name."

"Why, yes."

"What's his middle name?"

She hesitated a moment, then said, "Well, actually, Carter is the middle name. His first name is Edward, but he prefers the middle name, so he just signs everything Carter Gilman."

"I see," Mason said thoughtfully. "Now, can you tell me just what happened, please?"

"I don't like to say over the telephone," Muriell said, "but . . . Well, when I couldn't find him anywhere in the house I was very much alarmed. Then, after a while, I partially regained my composure and started cleaning up the dishes. Then I couldn't find his napkin. Wherever he'd gone he'd taken his napkin with him and so I went out to the workshop."

"What's the workshop?" Mason asked.

Muriell laughed nervously. "It's hard for me to explain, Mr. Mason. I'm so upset and I know it's hard for you to get a picture over the telephone, but his workshop is where he works at his hobby. He does woodworking and sometimes some modeling in clay. I'm out there now. A chair has been smashed and there's money all over the floor and a pool of—of blood."

"All right," Mason said, "you sit tight. I'm coming right out. I'll be there just as quick as I can make it— Have you said anything to anyone?"

"No."

"Don't say anything," Mason said. "Don't touch anything. Stay right there."

"Daddy's napkin is here on the floor," she said, "and—"

"You sit tight," Mason said, "I'll be right out. Don't touch anything. Now this workshop you mention is in a garage building in back of the house?"

"Yes."

"There's a driveway into the garage, of course. Is there a vacant stall in the garage where I can leave my car?"

"Yes."

"I'll be driving my car," Mason said. "I'll drive into the garage. You wait for me."

Mason glanced at Della Street. "You sit on the lid here, Della. I'm going out."

"What about this eleven-thirty appointment?"

"I'll be back for it," Mason said, "but I doubt very much if we're going to see Edward Carter."

Mason grabbed his hat, hurried down the corridor, took the elevator to the foyer, walked to the parking lot, jumped into his car and drove out into the congested morning traffic.

It took him twenty-five minutes to reach the address on Vauxman Avenue.

The lawyer turned into the driveway, noticed the big mansion which somehow seemed austerely silent. He drove into the garage and parked the car.

A door opened. A young woman twenty years old with brown hair, warm agate-colored eyes, and a good figure which radiated long-legged grace, stood in the doorway. She tried a wan smile.

"Mr. Mason?" she asked as the lawyer got out of his car.

Mason nodded. "You're Muriell Gilman?"

"Yes."

"Is this the workshop?"

"No, this is Nancy's darkroom—my stepmother's darkroom."

"And the sports car?" Mason asked, indicating a car in the middle section of the garage.

"That's mostly for Glamis and me, but sometimes Nancy uses it. The other car, the club coupé, is a family car."

"Are the rest of the family up?" Mason asked.

"Not a sound out of them," Muriell said. "They usually sleep until noon."

"Let's take a look," Mason said.

"If you'll follow me, please," Muriell said. "I'd better lead the way."

She moved back into the darkroom. Mason, following her, noticed the shadowy outlines of photographic enlarging cameras, of a developing sink, of a printing box and filing cabinets.

"If you'll just stand by that door and hold it open until I open the other door," she said, "we won't need to turn on the lights."

Mason stood by the door waiting.

Muriell crossed to the other door, opened it, and said, "This is Daddy's workshop."

Mason looked inside, then took Muriell by the shoulders and gently moved her back beside him so that they stood in the darkroom looking at the interior of the workshop.

There were lathes, saws, sanders and other woodworking machinery. Strung along rafters over the room were bits of rare wood carefully arranged so that all surfaces were exposed to the air. There were other slabs of wood on the workbench. The place was redolent with the odor of cedar, of sandalwood and the aroma of finely powdered sawdust.

The red stain formed a glaring oasis among the hundred-dollar bills carpeting the floor.

"This is the napkin your father was using?" Mason asked.

"Yes."

"You're sure?" Mason asked.

"Well . . . a napkin was missing, and this is one of our napkins."

Mason bent and picked up the piece of linen, said, "There are some egg stains here."

"I'm sure it's Daddy's, Mr. Mason. He had eggs and homemade venison sausage for breakfast."

"How many eggs?"

"Two."

"How many pieces of sausage?"

"There were two big slabs of sausage."

"It was put up in the style of a country sausage?"

"That's right, then frozen and thawed out for cooking."

"What else did your father have?"

"Cereal, toast and coffee."

"Any juice?"

"Yes, orange juice."

Mason inspected the napkin carefully, then thoughtfully folded it and slipped it in the side pocket of his coat.

"Then your father said he was still hungry?"

"He asked me if I'd mind cooking him another egg and another piece of sausage."

"That took a few minutes?"

"Quite a few minutes because the sausage was still so frozen I had to cut it in the center with a meat saw."

"I see," Mason said. He moved across the cement floor to study the sinister red spot. While he was making his investigation, Muriell kept talking, telling him about her father, the events of the morning.

The lawyer listened to her carefully, then bent over the red spot. He looked puzzled for a moment, then gently touched his finger to the thick liquid. He rubbed thumb and finger together, smelled and said, "That's not blood. That's some kind of red enamel."

"Oh, for heaven's sake!" Muriell said. "Are you sure?"

"I'm sure," Mason said, looking around, "and there's the can of enamel there on the shelf."

Muriell started over toward the can. "Just a minute," Mason warned. "Let's not leave any fingerprints on that can, if you don't mind, Muriell. That can has been upset and then it's been picked up again. . . . You don't have any idea *when* it was upset?"

She shook her head.

"Or, of course, when the chair was broken?"

"No, but there must have been a struggle and—"

"A struggle, surely," Mason interrupted, "but we don't know *when* that struggle took place, Miss Gilman; and we mustn't jump at conclusions. It could be that your father entered the room and saw the can of paint lying on its side, and the broken chair, and decided to pick up the can of paint. You see, it's a can of enamel with a small slip-on cap. The cap was loose. In all probability not all of the enamel drained out. However, I don't want to touch the can to find out. Let's be rather careful not to leave any fingerprints."

"There must be some of my fingerprints here," Muriell said. "I'm out here all the time. I come out to watch Daddy work."

"I see," Mason said. "However, I think it's better if we don't leave any *fresh* fingerprints. They might be superimposed on some other fingerprints. Let's pick up this money and count it. Tell me details while we're working."

Together they picked up the hundred-dollar bills and Mason put them together in a sheaf. Then he turned to Muriell "How many did you pick up?"

"Forty-eight."

"Then," Mason said, "there are exactly a hundred of these bills, making an even ten thousand dollars. Do you know anything about that or have any idea where the money could have come from?"

She shook her head.

"How about some rubber bands?" Mason said.

"There are some in Nancy's darkroom. I know where she keeps them."

"All right, let's get some rubber bands."

Muriell clicked on a light switch.

"Tut, tut!" Mason said, "I told you to be careful about touching things."

"Oh, I forgot— How am I going to get the rubber bands without leaving fingerprints?"

"Use a handkerchief or the hem of your skirt," Mason said.

She raised her skirt to take the hem in her hand and opened a drawer. The inside of the drawer was divided into partitions and each partition held rubber bands of a different size.

Mason used the tip of his fountain pen to lift out two rubber bands, then nodded to Muriell to close the drawer.

The lawyer slipped the rubber bands over the ends of the stack of currency.

"Your stepmother is quite a neat housekeeper," he said. "This place is quite the opposite of the confusion in your father's workshop."

"I know. Nancy is a fiend for order as far as the darkroom is concerned. I don't think she's quite so particular about housekeeping, but in her darkroom everything has to be perfectly spick-and-span and in apple-pie order."

"Your father is somewhat different?" Mason said.

She laughed. "If you refer to Daddy's workshop as being in apple-pie order, it would have to be an open-faced apple pie made with scrambled apples."

"I see," Mason said. "Now, do you have a picture of your father that you can get?"

"Why, yes, there's a framed portrait in my room but—"

"It might not be advisable for you to go to the house right at the moment," Mason said. "Are there any here in the darkroom?"

"Oh, yes, I guess there must be. Nancy has dozens of pictures. She likes to do portrait work. She has a technique by which she makes a very light image of the portrait on paper, then uses paints to build up and color the photograph until it looks like a regular oil painting. Unless you studied it closely you wouldn't realize that it had a photographic base."

"Then there should be some photographs of your father here," Mason said. "Let's see if we can find one without touching anything."

They moved around the darkroom. At length Muriell said, "I think there are some in this drawer."

She bent down to clutch the edge of her skirt between thumb and forefinger before opening the drawer.

"Yes," she said, "here are several."

"We'll just take this top one," Mason said, taking an eight-by-ten enlargement from the top of the drawer. "Now, that's your father?"

"Yes, that's Daddy. The lighting is a little flat and the image is printed rather light on the paper because that's the way Nancy likes to work, but that's Daddy, all right."

Mason studied the rounded face with some interest. "How old is he?"

"Well, let's see, Daddy's forty-two or maybe it's forty-three."

"And your stepmother?"

"Heavens knows," she said, laughing. "She's in the late thirties but she'll never tell you her age and we never ask."

"How old is Nancy's daughter, Glamis?"

"She's just twenty."

"And you?"

"I'm just the same age. . . . Mr. Mason, what are we going to do about Daddy? He must have taken the sedan. Should we trace it?"

Mason said, "I'll call you back a little after noon. I'll try and find out something. Your father has an office here in the city?"

"Oh, yes."

"Where?"

"In the Piedmont Building."

"What does he do?"

"He has an investment business, buying and selling properties, both for himself and for a list of clients who form investment pools."

"He's in the business by himself?"

"Well, I guess Daddy owns the business but there is an associate in with him."

"And have you telephoned the office to see if your father is there?"

"I telephoned about . . . well, shortly before I called you, and they said he was expected in at any time. I left word for him to call me when he came in. I wanted to tell him about his brief case."

Mason said, "Well, I'll try and get a line on things and let you know a little after noon. In the meantime, I don't think there's anything to worry about. You'd better take custody of this ten thousand dollars."

She seemed in a sudden panic. "Oh, no, Mr. Mason. I don't want to touch it. I don't know where that money came from. I don't know what this is all about and . . . well, now that I know that red pool is just red enamel on the cement I feel terribly sheepish about this whole business. I guess I acted like a fool, dragging you all the way out here.

"But I do want you to know, Mr. Mason, that I'll pay your bill, whatever it is. I have an individual checking account and . . . I guess I just went into a panic when I saw the money and the smashed chair and Daddy's napkin and the red pool in the middle of the floor."

"I can understand how you felt," Mason said. "I think everything's going to be all right. Just don't say anything about my having been here, and I'll just drive back to the office. Now remember, you're not to say a thing about the fact I was here—not to *anyone*. Do you understand?"

She nodded.

"At least not until after I've telephoned you," Mason said, "and I'll call you shortly after noon. You'll be here?"

"I most certainly will."

"All right," Mason told her, "I'll call you."

Back in his office, Mason reported to Della Street. "Put this sheaf of currency in the safe, Della. Here's an eight-by-ten enlargement of Mr. Carter Gilman and, for your information, the sinister red spot on the floor turned out to be the contents of a can of red enamel which had been turned over.

"Carter Gilman had evidently taken the sedan to work. Usually he walks four blocks to a bus stop. This morning he got up, left the house without a word, and took the sedan, unless he . . ."

"Unless he what?" she demanded.

"Looked in his workshop, found an intruder, had a fight, spilled ten thousand dollars in currency on the floor and then was taken for a ride while he was unconscious.

"And in that event, whoever returns to look for the ten grand will perhaps have a little difficulty finding it."

"Perhaps not too great difficulty," Della Street said.

"You may wind up as the target for an enterprising gunman."

"We'll have to take a chance on that," Mason said. "We have approximately half an hour before that appointment."

Della Street eyed Mason's desk. "You'll only have time to skim through the important letters on top of the pile."

"Okay," Mason said. "Then at eleven-thirty we'll take a good look at Mr. Edward Carter Gilman and find out just why he should have made an appointment under an assumed name."

"Since he was reading the paper," Della Street said, "do you want me to take a look on the financial page and see if I can get a clue?"

"It probably would be time wasted," Mason told her. "We don't know what his particular investments are and it wouldn't do any good just to make a blind stab. After all," he said, laughing, "a man gets up from breakfast and leaves in a hurry for his office. People do that every day. Hundreds of people, millions of people. We live at a rapid tempo."

"I know," Della Street rejoined, "but somehow the picture of that fried egg and the special homemade venison sausage on the plate . . ."

"Della," he said, "you're hungry. What did *you* have for breakfast?"

"Dry toast and coffee," she said. "I got on the scales yesterday and—"

"That's it," Perry Mason said. "You're hungry. Let's tackle this mail and forget Edward Carter Gilman until eleven-thirty."

CHAPTER THREE

As Perry Mason more or less surreptitiously looked at his watch for the fifth time within ten minutes, Della Street smiled and said, "Don't try to pull the wool over *my* eyes. You're all worked up about that appointment, wondering if he's going to show up or not."

"It is now four and a half minutes past eleven thirty, Della."

"At the sound of the chime," Della Street said.

Mason threw back his head and laughed. "All right, let's face it. I'm intrigued by this whole business."

"A father leaving the breakfast table without saying good-by to his daughter?" Della Street asked.

Mason shook his head. "A father eating two eggs and a couple of slabs of homemade venison sausage, then asking his daughter to go back to the kitchen and cook one more egg and another slab of sausage."

"Sounds like a working man," Della Street said.

Mason nodded.

"So then he takes ten thousand dollars and throws it all over the floor of his workshop," Della Street said.

"And drops his napkin, upsets a can of red paint and, having instructed his daughter not to call the police under any circumstances, leaves my name and telephone number for his daughter to find."

Della Street digested that information. "It sounds almost as if he might have planned to murder someone," she said.

"Now, as far as the food is concerned," Mason went on, "there is only one logical explanation. He had to get rid of her for a few moments. That was the only way he could think of to do it."

Della Street slowly nodded her head.

"In this day," Mason said, "with people conscious of diet and calories, that's quite a breakfast for anybody. But when you consider a man old enough to be the father of a grown girl eating a breakfast like that and then asking to have another egg and another slab of sausage—*and* not being there when the food comes to the table—the only logical explanation is that he wanted his daughter out of the way."

"Why?"

"Heaven knows. It may have been because of something he read in the paper. It may be because of something he saw out of the window."

"Now *that's* a thought!" Della Street said. "He . . ."

The phone on Della Street's desk rang.

Della picked up the receiver, said to the receptionist, "Yes, Gertie," then turned to Mason and smiled. "Mr. *Edward* Carter is here for his appointment."

"Have him come right in," Mason said.

"I'll bring him," Della Street said, hanging up the telephone and moving with supple grace to the door which led to the outer offices.

Mason watched her approvingly as she walked through the door, then got to his feet as Della ushered in a somewhat chubby man who looked as though he were somewhere in his forties.

"Mr. Mason," he said, "I'm sorry I'm late."

"Edward Carter," Della Street introduced.

There could be no question that this man was the man who had posed for the eight-by-ten photograph Muriell Gilman had given Perry Mason earlier in the day.

"Sometimes it's rather difficult to estimate traffic problems," Mason said. "I usually try to get to my appointments about five or ten minutes early and that leaves me a cushion in case of a traffic jam."

"Is that a subtle rebuke?" the man asked.

Mason smiled and shook his head. "Just a comment concerning my own personal habits. I seldom have time to be subtle. You wanted to consult me professionally, Mr. Carter?"

"Yes."

"Of course," Mason said, "I'm not certain I'm at liberty to accept you as a client. An attorney always has to be careful to screen his potential clients so as to make certain he doesn't get conflicting interests. So perhaps before you tell me the particulars you had better tell me generally what it's all about. Now, my secretary has your address as 6231 Vauxman Avenue— Is that right?"

"That's right. That's where I'm staying at the moment."

"Your business address?"

The man hesitated a moment, then shook his head and said, "I don't have any. I've sort of—sort of retired."

"All right," Mason said, "what is it generally that you want to see me about?"

"I am acting on behalf of a friend," the man said.

"Go on."

"This is a very dear friend, a woman who happens to be married to a man who is also a friend of mine."

"Her name?"

"Gilman. Nancy Gilman. I am visiting her and her husband at the moment. They are the ones who reside at 6231 Vauxman Avenue."

"I see," Mason said, his face expressionless. "Go on. What about Mrs. Gilman?"

"Mrs. Gilman is being blackmailed."

"You're certain?"

"Quite certain."

"And, as a friend, you want me to do something about it?"

"Let's take it one step at a time, Mr. Mason. One can't do very much with blackmail until he knows exactly what it is the person is being blackmailed about."

"And you have an idea?" Mason asked.

"Frankly, no. That's one of the things I want to find out."

"What else?"

"That's all for the present. After we find out what's in her past we'll probably know the hold that the blackmailer has over her."

"Do you, by any chance, know the blackmailer?"

"Yes."

"Who is it?" Mason asked, his voice showing his keen interest.

The man hesitated a moment, then said, "After all, I guess I have to be fair with you, Mr. Mason, and put my cards on the table. The blackmailer is a private detective named Vera Martel. Her middle initial is M. Her business cards and stationery simply state the name as 'V.M. Martel, Investigator.' There is nothing on her stationery or on her business cards to indicate that she's a woman. She has offices both here and in Las Vegas, Nevada. She seems to specialize in divorce business.

"That is to say, most of the clients who consult her are interested in divorce cases, one way or another."

"Just what do you want me to do?" Mason asked.

The man took an envelope from his coat pocket, said, "I prefer to handle things of this nature on a strictly cash basis, Mr. Mason. I have here seven hundred and fifty dollars."

He reached a well-manicured hand into the envelope, took out a five-hundred-dollar bill, two one-hundred-dollar bills and a fifty-dollar bill. "You'll want some money for expenses. You'll need a private detective agency and also a retainer," the man said.

Mason didn't move to pick up the money. "You'll be staying here in the city for some time?"

"Long enough for this matter to terminate, I hope."

"And if I want to reach you I can simply call the Gilman residence?"

"Heavens! Don't call me there!"

"How can I get in touch with you, then?"

"I—I'd better call you. I certainly wouldn't like to have the folks I'm visiting think that I . . . well, even as an intimate friend of the family . . . I don't want to seem to be interfering in their affairs."

"I see. You expect to be visiting there for some time?"

"Yes. However, *don't* try to get in touch with me there. I'll call you."

Mason studied the man, looked at the slightly chunky

figure, the bushy eyebrows, the patient, thoughtful brown eyes behind tortoise-shell glasses, the long wisp of hair which was coiled around the bald spot on the top of the man's head.

"You're there during the day?" Mason asked.

The man became impatient. "I tell you, Mr. Mason, *I'll* get in touch with *you*. Please don't try to get in touch with me."

"I'm just trying to find out something about the arrangement there," Mason said, "before I can tell whether or not I'm going to take the case."

"I see. Well, I can explain it very simply, Mr. Mason. I'm an old friend, a very old friend, of Mr. Gilman. Mr. Gilman was married rather happily. He has one daughter, Muriell. She is twenty years of age. She's living there in the house.

"Mr. Gilman's first wife was killed in an automobile accident and he married again. Nancy, his present wife, had a daughter by a prior marriage. Her name is Glamis—Glamis Barlow. She's the same age as Gilman's daughter—twenty. They're a delightful family.

"I am very fond of the entire family. The two daughters are exemplary. They are as different in tastes and background as can be, but in loyalty and affection they are as alike as two yolks in an egg.

"One is rather demure but smart as chain lightning; that's Muriell Gilman. The other is verbally daring, quick at repartee, but intensely devoted to her friends and exceedingly loyal. That's Glamis Barlow.

"I certainly wouldn't want anything to happen that would blight their lives. They are, to use a trite expression, on the threshold of happiness."

"You're very fond of these girls?"

"I love them. They are devoted daughters, estimable young women. Despite differences of complexion and mannerisms they are duplicate and intensely devoted daughters."

"But it is Mrs. Gilman who is being blackmailed?"

"I believe so, but it could very well have something to do with either one or the other daughter."

"What does Mr. Gilman do?" Mason asked.

"Investments. He buys property, develops it, sells it—has rather a shrewd eye for real estate. He also manages investment pools."

"You've known him for a long time?"

"A very long time."

"And what about his present wife?"

"She's an artist—that is, she has artistic tendencies. She likes to paint and she's very much interested in photography. Right at the moment she's experimenting with portrait work. She takes photographic portraits and prints them very lightly on enlarging paper. Then she colors the portrait. The photograph is little more than an outline and by the time she gets done she has a very interesting oil painting."

"She does this commercially?"

"Heavens no. It's just a fad. She's . . . well, I think she's rather well fixed."

"They set a good table?" Mason asked casually.

"*Very* good—although I don't see what that has to do with it."

"They sound like a family that appreciates the good things of life."

"They do."

"I like to eat, myself," Mason said, "but I've reached a point where I have to watch my calories—not enough outdoor exercise."

"I know," his visitor said. "People are supposed to keep from putting on too much weight. I'm supposed to watch mine, too."

"I like a good breakfast," Mason said.

"So do I."

"Quite frequently I pass up lunch."

"I do, too."

"But you do have trouble with your weight?" Mason asked.

"Oh, yes. I have to watch myself."

"What's a typical breakfast?" Mason asked.

"Oh, toast and soft-boiled eggs, perhaps, sometimes a fried egg. What's the reason for this, Mr. Mason?"

"Just trying to get the picture," Mason said breezily. "What's Gilman's first name, by the way?"

"Carter."

"Oh," Mason said, "the same as your last name. You're not any relation, are you?"

"No."

"Can you describe Mr. Gilman?"

"Why, he's—he's about my age. He's . . . well, when you come right down to it, it's rather hard to give a physical description of a person—a friend . . . let's see . . . but you mustn't ever try to reach him."

Mason's visitor leaned back and closed his eyes. "I'm trying to visualize him," he said.

"Oh, well, never mind," Mason said. "I think I have the picture pretty well. I was just trying to make sure that you weren't being officious and butting into something that would cause hard feelings. But I guess it's all right. By the way, does Mr. Gilman know that you're calling on me?"

"No. He has no idea. I'm doing this on my own."

"And you want me to check into Mrs. Gilman's past and find out what it is that would lay her open to blackmail?"

The man nodded.

"That's rather a difficult and an expensive way of going at it," Mason said. "Wouldn't it be a little better to try and check on this Martel woman and see if we couldn't find out what she's working on?"

Carter's shake of the head was emphatic. "I want you to start working on Nancy Gilman," he said. "Go back to the Year One. Find out everything you can about her."

"Well, what do we have to start on?" Mason asked. "Where was she born, how old is she?"

"She's thirty-nine. She was born in Los Angeles. I don't know too much about her marriage to Steve Barlow. I gathered that it was just an average marriage. She was young at the time and—"

"He died?" Mason asked.

"No, they were divorced."

"Where were they married?"

"In San Francisco. Barlow worked in San Francisco. He was in the insurance business, I believe."

"Has he remarried, do you know?"

"I don't know. I rather think he has."

"Where does he live? Do you know?"

"Las Vegas, Nevada."

"Do you have the address?"

"No. As a friend of the family, I'd hardly have that."

"Does this daughter ever visit him, or does he ever visit her?"

"I believe Glamis does see something of him. I think she visits him in Las Vegas. However, Mr. Mason, I can tell you very positively all this has nothing to do with what I want to find out. I want to know about Nancy's past, what there is in it which could possibly cause her to pay blackmail."

"There might be many things," Mason said drily.

The man shook his head. "You don't know Nancy. If someone raked up a purple chapter out of her past, Nancy would simply laugh it off. She'd admit it and even furnish more details—and she'd get away with it. She's that type: vital, magnetic, unconventional.

"But this thing, whatever it is, has her worried sick. I can't imagine what it could be unless it's a—well, a murder."

"You think it might be that?" Mason asked.

"I can't think of anything else that would cause her such concern as this has."

Mason said, "Well, I'll see what I can find out. I will, of course, have to use a detective agency—you suggested that."

His visitor nodded. "You have a good private detective, Mr. Mason, one you use and can trust?"

"I do. The Drake Detective Agency here in the building, with offices on the same floor. I'll call in Paul Drake and start him working."

The man looked at his watch. "I've taken up more than the time you allotted, Mr. Mason. I am sorry. I'll be on my way."

He got to his feet.

"You wouldn't care to meet Paul Drake?" Mason asked. "He might have some questions."

"No, thank you, Mr. Mason. Some other time, perhaps, but all Mr. Drake needs to do is to check into the past of Nancy Gilman, find out everything he can about her and, if possible, find out why she should be afraid of a blackmailer."

"You're satisfied she's being blackmailed?"

"I'm virtually positive."

"Does her husband know?"

"Heavens, no."

"Can you tell me something about the house they live in?"

The man's eyes narrowed slightly. "Is *that* important?"

"Just a general description of the place," Mason said.

"Well, it's a big, rather old-fashioned, three-story house. It has a large attic, I understand, although I haven't been up there."

"A basement?"

"Oh, yes. One that's used for a furnace and air-conditioning unit. Mr. Gilman has a workshop at the back of the house where he does woodwork for a hobby. He has some lathes and saws and likes to make little jewel cases for his friends, and then there's a darkroom adjoining this workshop where Nancy does her developing and enlarging."

"Rather a large building in back?"

"Yes. It was made for a three-car garage and living quarters for a chauffeur."

"Well, thank you very much," Mason said. "We'll get at it. You don't want me to try to get in touch with you no matter what happens, is that right?"

"It might prove embarrassing. *I'll* be in touch with *you,* Mr. Mason."

"So far, Mr. Carter," Mason said, "you haven't presented any problem that calls for the services of an attorney. You have only asked for information which could be gathered by a private detective. I think it would be much better for you to go to Mr. Paul Drake and retain him as a detective. There's no use retaining an attorney simply to get information which, in the long run, will have to be supplied by a private detective anyway."

"No, no," the man said hastily, "you don't understand me. I want you as an attorney."

"Just what do you want me to do as an attorney?"

"I want you to represent . . . well, I want you to represent the family."

"The family?"

"Yes. All of the family."

"Who, in particular?"

"Nancy Gilman, Carter Gilman, Muriell Gilman and Glamis Barlow."

"All of them?"

"Yes."

"Suppose they should have conflicting interests?"

"They won't have."

"But suppose they should have?"

"Then you are at liberty to withdraw from the case and keep the retainer I have given you."

"Suppose some member of the family should have interests that conflict with yours?"

"They won't."

Mason said abruptly, "Mr. Gilman has this workshop

back of the house adjoining the darkroom, a shop where he does woodworking?"

"That's right. He also does clay modeling."

"And you're visiting there?"

"Yes."

"Do you own any part of the material in that workshop?"

"No, of course not. I own nothing there. I am simply a visitor, a friend of the family."

"And as a friend you want to retain me to represent the family?"

"In case anyone in the family needs representation, but primarily I want you to find out what it is in Nancy Gilman's past that would lay her open to blackmail."

Mason said, "That's a very unusual request and I'll give you a very unusual answer, Mr. Carter."

"What's that?"

"I want you to pay me the retainer of seven hundred and fifty dollars. In addition to that, I want you to assign to me all your right, title and interest, whatever it may be, to any of the contents of the workshop in the garage building as those contents exist at the present time or existed any time during the day."

"But that's absurd, Mr. Mason. I've told you I don't own anything in that workshop."

"Nevertheless," Mason said, "that is the only condition on which I can undertake to represent you in the matter."

"Will you kindly tell me why in the name of reason you have put such a price on your services?"

"If you don't own anything there," Mason said, "it isn't a price. I am simply asking you to sign over all of your right, title and interest to anything that is in there. If you don't have any right, any title or any interest, you aren't signing over anything."

"Are you trying to trap me or trick me, Mr. Mason?"

"Certainly not," Mason said. "I am trying to protect myself."

"Can you tell me one good reason why I should do that?"

"Can you tell me one good reason why you shouldn't?" Mason asked.

"Look here, Mr. Mason, I simply must have your services. I want to have the assurance that, no matter what happens, you will protect that family, each and every member of that family. If you find their interests come in conflict you may withdraw . . . but I want you to be certain that there is a real conflict, not just an apparent conflict. I want you to do everything you can for every member of that family because I think perhaps they are going to go through some critical times."

Mason said, "I understand. I want a seven-hundred-and-fifty-dollar retainer and I want you to assign to me all of your right, title and interest in and to all of the contents of the workshop."

"Very well," the man said angrily, "prepare your assignment. I'll sign it. You leave me no choice in the matter."

Mason nodded to Della Street, said, "Take a bill of sale, Della, and make it out for Mr. Carter to sign."

Della Street took one of the forms, vanished from the office, returned in a few moments and handed the form to Mason's visitor.

The man signed "Edward Carter" in a bold vertical handwriting.

"Sign as a witness, Della," Mason said.

Della Street signed as a witness.

"Now, I'm not to get in touch with you," Mason said. "You're going to get in touch with me?"

"That's right."

"And, by the same sign, if anything happens that requires me to represent any of the family, shall I get in touch with them?"

"Wait for them to get in touch with you," the man said. "They will if the situation requires."

"Thank you very much, Mr. Carter," Mason said, shaking hands. "Della Street will give you a receipt for the seven hundred and fifty dollars, which, plus the assignment, will act as a retainer."

"I still don't see the reason for that bill of sale," the man protested.

Mason's smile was enigmatic. "I still don't see the reason for your visit."

"All right," the man said. "I'll ride along with you. I know your reputation, Mr. Mason; in fact, I've looked it up rather carefully."

"Thank you," Mason said.

The man left the office after accepting the receipt Della Street handed him.

"Well?" Mason asked as the door closed.

Della Street shook her head. "How I'd like to know what he's holding back!"

"He's evidently holding back quite a lot," Mason said. "He's hardly the type who should have three eggs and three pieces of homemade venison sausage for breakfast."

"To say nothing of cereal, toast and several cups of coffee," Della Street pointed out. "Do you want Paul Drake?" she asked.

Mason nodded.

Della Street rang Drake's phone and relayed the request from Mason.

"May I ask why the bill of sale to the contents of the workshop?" Della Street asked.

Mason grinned. "If that ten thousand dollars lying on the floor of the workshop was money he'd collected to pay blackmail, I now have a legitimate excuse to hold it and can't be held for suppressing evidence."

While Della Street was digesting this information, Paul Drake gave his code knock at the side door of the office.

Della Street let him in.

"Another job for you," Mason said.

"Good," Drake said. "I had a bad day at the races. I need a job."

"Don't get too hungry on this one," Mason warned.

"What is it?"

"Nancy Gilman, 6231 Vauxman Avenue. You are to check into her past. She was born in Los Angeles, married a Steve Barlow in San Francisco, has a child named Glamis, rather a young woman by this time—twenty years old. Nancy divorced Steve Barlow, or he divorced her, and she's now married to Carter Gilman, who is, I believe, a free-lance speculator and makes his living out of investments. Steve Barlow lives in Las Vegas, Nevada. Glamis may visit him from time to time. There's another daughter, Muriell Gilman.

"Nancy is being blackmailed by a private detective named Vera M. Martel, who describes herself on her cards as V. M. Martel and—"

"Vera, eh?" Drake interrupted.

"You know her?" Mason asked.

"Like a book," Drake said.

"What about her?"

"She's around fifty, weighs about one hundred pounds soaking wet, has a long, thin mouth that seems to stretch from ear to ear, a prominent nose and narrow, close-set gimlet eyes. She talks like a house afire, she's smart as they come, and she's hell on wheels."

"Would she stoop to blackmail?"

"She'd blackmail," Drake said. "It wouldn't be stooping, it would be on her normal level. You might even say it would be reaching up."

"How does she keep her license?"

"Blackmail," Drake said.

"You didn't understand me. I asked how she kept her license."

"You didn't understand me," Drake said. "She keeps it by blackmail."

"How come?"

"No one prefers charges against her. Whenever she fleeces anyone she does it so cleverly, so shrewdly and so thoroughly that they wouldn't think of preferring charges. She looks around carefully before she gets ready to sink her fangs into a victim. She's like a spider sitting back patiently waiting in a corner of his web. He's capable of going for long periods of time without food, then when something gets tangled in his web he comes down, strikes swiftly and drains the victim dry. Vera is the same way."

"You're getting positively poetic, Paul," Mason said. "Nancy Gilman may be a victim and I've been retained to see that she gets out of the spider's web."

Drake gave a low whistle. "That's going to be a job," he said. "When you deal with Vera Martel you're dealing with dynamite. She's diabolically clever. She won't walk into any of your regular traps and if she's got something on Nancy Gilman you can gamble that she's got Nancy all tied up so that Nancy wouldn't dare to give us the slightest co-operation. How did it happen Nancy got nerve enough to come to you?"

"She didn't," Mason said. "It's a long story."

"Well?" Drake asked, lighting a cigarette. "Are you going to tell it?"

"No," Mason said. "Get out, and get busy on Nancy Gilman. Find out everything you can about her past and don't stick me for *too* big a bill because the traffic may not stand it."

Drake heaved himself out of the big chair. "On my way," he said, "but keep your eyes out for Vera, Perry, and let's hope she doesn't get her hooks in *you.* If she finds out you're on her back trail *she'll* dig into *your* past."

"I haven't got any," Mason said.

Paul Drake winked at Della Street and slipped out into the corridor.

Mason said to Della, "Ring up Muriell Gilman and tell her our investigation so far indicates that her father is physically safe. Tell her we can't give her any further details and that she is not to let her father know anything about the call."

CHAPTER FOUR

IT WAS about ten minutes before three o'clock that afternoon when the telephone rang and Della Street, answering it, said, "This is Miss Street, Mr. Mason's confidential secretary. . . . Who? . . . Can you tell me what it's about? . . . Just a minute, I'll see."

Della Street placed her hand over the mouthpiece of the telephone and said excitedly, "Vera M. Martel is on the line and she wants to talk with you concerning a matter which she says is very personal."

Mason said, "Listen in, Della."

He picked up the telephone on his desk and said, "Hello. This is Mr. Mason talking."

The woman's voice was rather high-pitched. She talked so rapidly that one word seemed to be treading on the heels of the next and made it difficult to understand what she was saying.

"Mr. Mason, I just wanted to warn you that people who butt into business that doesn't concern them usually find they have made a big mistake."

"Are you insinuating I'm butting into business that doesn't concern me?" Mason asked.

"Don't be silly," she said. "You've been retained by a man who gave the name of Edward Carter. For your information, that was E. Carter Gilman, the husband of

Nancy Gilman. Don't let him pull the wool over your eyes and don't think that you're going to step in and wave a magic wand and that the Gilman troubles will be over.

"I happen to know what I'm talking about. I just want to warn you that this is too complicated a matter for a simple solution, Mr. Mason. Carter Gilman is a fool. If he knew what he was stirring up he'd be the first to tell you to pocket the seven hundred and fifty dollars and forget the whole thing. I'm afraid poor Mr. Gilman is just a little stupid. He's bringing about the very trouble he's trying to avoid."

Mason glanced significantly at Della Street who was on the extension phone, her pencil flying over the page of the shorthand book.

The lawyer waited until the pencil came to a pause, signifying Della had caught up with the other woman's rapid delivery.

"Did you think that a phone call from you, Miss Martel, would be all that was necessary to make any lawyer at any time quit working for any client you might designate?"

"Of course not," she snapped. "I'm not foolish enough to waste my time or yours. Now, simply ring up Graystone 9-3535 and ask whoever answers the phone to connect you with Edward Carter. Tell him who you are and tell him Vera Martel rang you up and said to tell him, 'Your fingerprints are *over* those of the person you are trying to protect.' Do you understand, Mr. Mason? Simply give him that message. You aren't to tell him any more than that—and the number once more, Mr. Mason, is Graystone 9-3535—although I feel quite certain your very beautiful secretary is either taking this conversation down in shorthand or else it's being recorded on a tape recorder.

There's no need for any comment, Mr. Mason. Your client is a fool. Good-by!"

The phone slammed at the other end of the line.

Mason hung up and Della Street, who had been taking shorthand notes, slowly replaced her receiver.

"Well?" Mason asked.

"Good heavens, what a delivery!" Della Street said. "I guess I got all of it but it certainly was a job. She talked like a house afire. It seemed like she was going five hundred words a minute."

"Anything else?" Mason asked.

"Miss Martel seems to keep very well informed on what happens with the people whom she decides to blackmail."

"Doesn't she!" Mason said.

"Any idea how she does it?" Della Street asked.

"Not yet."

"And what about the fact that Edward Carter is really Carter Gilman?"

"That's not news, at least to us," Mason said.

"But how in the world could she know? He evidently gave you a name that he felt would throw you off the track just so she *wouldn't* find out, and here within—within four hours of the time he left the office she calls up to warn you to lay off."

"Well," Mason said, "we'll at least check her information. We owe that much to our client and to ourselves, Della. Call Graystone 9-3535 and ask for Mr. Carter."

"Won't that just be playing into her hands?" Della Street asked.

Mason grinned. "We're leading from the dummy, Della."

Della Street put through the call, asked for Mr. Carter, then nodded to Mason.

The lawyer picked up his phone. A moment later a voice sounding somewhat puzzled said, "Hello, who did you wish to speak with?"

"Mr. Carter?" Mason said. "This is Perry Mason, the lawyer."

"What!"

"Do you wish me to repeat? This is Perry Mason, the lawyer."

"Great heavens! . . . I told you not to try to call me. How in the world did you ever locate me here? What do you want?"

"Miss Martel just rang me up," Mason said. "She told me to call you at this number and say to you, and I quote, 'Your fingerprints are *over* those of the person you are trying to protect.'

"Now, does that message mean anything to you?"

There was a long period of silence.

"You there?" Mason asked.

The voice at the other end of the phone was shaken, all but inaudible. "I'm here . . . I'm trying to think . . . I . . . what have you done so far, Mr. Mason?"

"I have a detective agency working on the investigation. It has representatives here and in San Francisco digging up information."

The voice at the other end of the line suddenly snapped with decision. "Very well, Mr. Mason, I can see the matter is more serious than I supposed it was when I called on you. I'm going to have to change some of the instructions I gave you."

"Now just a minute," Mason said. "So far you're just a

voice over the telephone. I don't accept instructions that way. Can you identify yourself?"

"I am the man who called on you this morning, Mr. Mason. I gave you one five-hundred-dollar bill, two one-hundreds and a fifty. I have your receipt signed by Della Street, your secretary."

"You'll have to do better than that," Mason said. "Is there any other way you can identify yourself?"

"Good heavens, Mason, this is a serious matter. Isn't it enough that I have given you a substantial retainer and that you have accepted it?"

"Since you ask the question," Mason said, "I'll answer it. The answer is: No, that isn't enough. I want definite identification."

"All right," the man said, "I suppose I'll have to come clean. My real name *is* Carter Gilman. I made the appointment with you as Edward Carter. When I came to your office I told you I was a little late and you told me that traffic conditions being what they were, you always found it advisable to try to get to your appointments a few minutes early and then, if you were held up, the other man wasn't kept waiting.

"Your secretary sat on your right-hand side at a little desk of her own with a telephone on it and took notes. She handed me the receipt immediately after you and I had shaken hands when I was leaving."

"How were you dressed?" Mason asked.

"I had on a brown suit, a gray tie with red bars on a diagonal. I wore brown and white sports shoes and tortoise-shell glasses; that is, the so-called horn-rimmed glasses.

"Mr. Mason, the message which you have just given me

has come as a distinct shock because it means that persons whom I thought I could trust are arrayed against me. I now admit my identity. I *am* Carter Gilman.

"I am going to give you detailed instructions which are very important and which must be followed to the letter. My daughter, Muriell, I can trust. She is very much upset over the manner in which I left the house this morning. She has driven to my office in the Piedmont Building and is making discreet inquiries of my secretary, Matilda Norman. I am going to telephone her to put her mind at ease and I am going to give her certain specific instructions. She will go at once to your office in carrying out those instructions and tell you just what you are to do.

"I want you to accept Muriell's instructions just as though they came directly from me. She will tell you some things that are so highly confidential I don't dare discuss them over the telephone.

"And, Mr. Mason, please do not underestimate Vera Martel. The fact that she knew I could be reached at this number at this particular time is very disturbing. The message which she gave you is one that was designed to get me to run for cover and call this whole thing off. Now that the situation is out in the open, now that she knows I have consulted you, now that she knows we are headed for a showdown, I am going to come out in the open and start fighting.

"I will no longer masquerade as Edward Carter, a friend of the family. If you will wait there at your office you will hear from my daughter, Muriell, within the next ten minutes. It shouldn't take her longer than that to get to your office. Please do everything she says."

"Now just a minute," Mason said. "You're dealing the

cards pretty fast here, Gilman. You wanted me to try and find out something about Mrs. Gilman. Now suddenly you're changing all of the instructions and dumping an entirely different case in my lap."

"Well, does it make any difference what I ask you to do, just so I pay you for doing it, Mr. Mason?"

"It may make a whale of a difference," Mason said. "And what you want me to do now may cost a lot more money than what you wanted me to do this morning."

Gilman said, "Very well, Mr. Mason. I will see that you are paid. Remember that I not only gave you a retainer of seven hundred and fifty dollars, but you wanted title to all of the machinery and personal property that was in my workshop. I don't know what put that particular idea in your mind, but I can now tell you, Mr. Mason, that if you will drive out with Muriell to that workshop you will find a large sum of money on the floor. That money should serve as additional compensation until you can hear from me again.

"Please wait right there until you hear from Muriell."

The telephone connection was severed at the other end.

Mason looked quizzically at Della Street.

"Well?" she asked, as she hung up the telephone.

Mason said, "This could be a beautifully engineered trap. A man comes in and tells me he's a friend of the family, he wants a routine investigation made. Prior to that time his daughter has been in touch with me and has me go out to the house, where I pick up ten thousand dollars in hundred-dollar bills. Then, having inveigled me into that situation up to my neck, so to speak, they suddenly change the instructions and tell me what else to do."

"And what are you going to do?" Della Street asked.

"I don't know," Mason said. "It depends on what Muriell has in mind when she shows up. Somehow I don't think Muriell can carry out very much of a deception. If this is some elaborate scheme that she and her father have entered into, I think I can break Muriell down. But I certainly hate to pick on her. I'd much rather have had Carter Gilman come in here and give me a chance to probe *his* mind."

"Which is undoubtedly why Carter Gilman has no intention of coming in," Della Street said.

"I guess there's no doubt about that being Gilman," Mason said.

"No doubt on earth," Della Street assured him. "I listened carefully to the voice. That's the voice of the man who was in here this morning."

Mason regarded her thoughtfully. "And just how do we know that man is Carter Gilman?" he asked.

"You have his photograph," Della Street said. "You had his photograph before he came in."

"That's right," Mason said, "I have his photograph. And where did I get his photograph?"

"From his daughter."

"That's right," Mason said. "Out at his house. Muriell opens a drawer in the darkroom. Very conveniently there is a photograph of her father there. She tells me that this is a photograph of her father, that her father has mysteriously disappeared. She ushers me into a room where there is ten thousand dollars on the floor. I pick up the ten thousand dollars and come back here to the office. The man whose photograph I have seen comes walking in and tells me he is a friend of the family. I walk right into the trap and pull the cat-and-mouse act with him and he's probably getting quite a kick out of it. The whole thing has probably been rehearsed with him and his daughter.

"Now he lets me locate him on the phone after having a telephone conversation with a woman who says she is Vera Martel. . . . How the devil do I know that was Vera Martel I was talking with? How do I know that I'm not being swept along in a stream of events where Muriell gives me a picture and says that's her father, where her father rings me up and tells me to do exactly what Muriell says, and where some other person rings me up and says she is Vera Martel and gives me one of these mysterious, thoroughly cockeyed messages to pass on to Carter Gilman?

"So far, about all I have are voices over the telephone and a photograph handed me by Muriell."

"I would say a great deal depends on Muriell," Della Street said thoughtfully.

Mason said, "All right, Della. Vera Martel is a private detective who has offices here and in Las Vegas. Get her on the phone."

"What will we do when we get her, Chief?"

"I'll ask her what the hell she meant by ringing up my office and telling me something about fingerprints."

"And suppose she denies the conversation?"

"We'll have a chance to listen to her voice," Mason said. "You have a good ear for voices. You can identify them quite accurately over the telephone."

"I'm quite certain I can identify Vera Martel's voice," Della Street said. "At least the woman who said she was Vera Martel."

"All right," Mason said, "get busy. Call Vera Martel. If she isn't in her office find out where she can be reached.

If she can be reached anywhere in the country by telephone I want her."

Mason started pacing the floor while Della Street went out to the outer office to put the calls through the office switchboard.

Fifteen minutes later Della Street returned. "Vera Martel's office doesn't know where she is. Apparently they would like very much to find out. They gave me the number of her Las Vegas office. I called there. There was no answer."

"No secretary there?" Mason asked.

"Apparently not. From what Vera Martel's office here told me, the office in Las Vegas is one that is kept for the convenience of Miss Martel and her clients. Miss Martel remains there when she's in Las Vegas. The secretary here seems very much disturbed. Vera Martel was working on an important case and she seems to have disappeared."

"Makes it quite a day for disappearances, doesn't it?" Mason said.

"It does indeed."

The phone on Della Street's desk rang and Della Street picked up the instrument, said, "Yes, Gertie, what is it?"

Della turned to Perry Mason and said, "Muriell Gilman is in the office."

"Tell her to come right in," Mason said grimly.

Muriell entered the office and said, almost as soon as Della Street had ushered her through the door, "Oh, Mr. Mason, I'm *so* relieved. I've heard from Daddy and he had to leave this morning on a very delicate, difficult matter. He's in some sort of trouble and he needs my help and he wants me to work with you."

"Did you tell him you'd called me earlier in the day?" Mason asked.

"No," she said. "You told me not to, and I—I didn't, although I probably would have if he'd have talked longer, but Daddy reached me on the telephone and said he only had time to give me a few very brief instructions."

"All right," Mason said. "First let's have the instructions."

"I was at Daddy's office trying to locate him or, failing in that, to talk with Tillie Norman, his secretary."

"Describe her," Mason said. "Young, attractive, curvaceous or . . . ?"

"Heavens no! She's very young-looking for her age and very competent, but I know she's well past fifty and she's not at all curvaceous. She's rather the beanpole type."

"All right," Mason said, "pardon me if I interrupt you with questions from time to time, but you're talking to a lawyer and I have to have a clear picture in my mind. Go on and tell me the rest of it."

"Daddy called in almost as soon as Tillie came in . . . she'd been out on a shopping trip. He learned I was there and told Tillie to have me put on the phone without letting anyone in the office know he had called in.

"Something had happened which upset Daddy very much indeed, something in connection with a telephone message which he told me you would know all about. He said that he's in a very precarious position. He said I was to come here just as fast as I could and that you were to accompany me out to the house, that I was to give you his brief case—he had left it home—that there were documents in that brief case, that you were to go directly to his office and surrender those documents to Roger C. Calhoun, his business associate, and accept Mr. Calhoun's receipt for the documents."

"Did he describe the documents?"

"Simply the agreements that were in the green Bristol-board folder in his brief case. He said that you were also to tell Mr. Calhoun that you were acting as Daddy's attorney and that Mr. Calhoun was to go ahead and complete negotiations on the agreements and execute them."

"Was I supposed to read the agreements?" Mason asked.

"Daddy didn't say anything about that."

Mason said, "Look, Muriell, I don't like to be brought into a situation where I'm groping in the dark. I'm a lawyer. If your father wants me to represent him in a business transaction, that's fine. If he wants me to try and head off blackmail, that's fine. If he wants me to protect your interests, that's fine.

"But I want to know what it is I'm supposed to do, and I want to work out my own plan of campaign. I don't want to be a legal messenger-boy who tries to do the things that your father thinks should be done. If he'll come to me with the problem I'll work out a solution of the problem with him. But I don't want to be sent around doing this and doing that in accordance with some plan *he's* worked out. Do you understand that?"

"I can appreciate your position," she said, her eyes clouding and seemingly close to tears, "but, Mr. Mason, my father would never want you to do anything that was the least bit wrong; and he's in some sort of serious trouble."

"Will you get hold of him and tell him that I want to

have some cards put on the table before I go running around here doing a lot of things that—?"

"Mr. Mason, *please,*" she said. "There won't be time. Daddy told Tillie to make an appointment with Mr. Calhoun. He's going to wait for you. We'll just about have time to run out and get those papers in the brief case and then deliver them to Mr. Calhoun and take his receipt—and there's a lot that I'm to tell you about Mr. Calhoun. Daddy said I was to tell you everything. I'll have to do that while we're driving out to the house."

Mason glanced at Della Street, frowned thoughtfully for a minute.

Muriell impatiently looked at her wristwatch.

"Where's your father's office?" Mason asked.

"In the Piedmont Building."

"That's only a couple of blocks from here," Mason said.

She nodded.

"Where's your car?"

"I parked it in the parking lot next to this building."

"All right," Mason said abruptly. "I'll go this far with you. I'll go down and get my car. I'll drive you out to the house and then you can ride back with me and pick up your car. You can tell me what it's all about while we're going out to the house. I'm going to ask you lots of questions, Muriell. Do you understand?"

"Yes. Daddy said I was to tell you everything."

Mason glanced at Della Street and said, "You stay on the job until I get back, Della. I'll probably go directly to the Piedmont Building and see Mr. Calhoun before I get back to the office."

Mason opened the exit door of his private office. "Come on," he said to Muriell, "let's go."

CHAPTER FIVE

PERRY MASON, driving his car through traffic, said, "Muriell, I'm going to have to keep my eyes pretty much on the road—do you understand?"

"Why, yes, of course, Mr. Mason."

"But," the lawyer said, "my ears are going to be concentrated on you, listening to your words, your tone of voice and waiting to detect any false note."

"Why should there be a false note, Mr. Mason?"

"I don't know," the lawyer said. "I just want to tell you that I've cross-examined a lot of witnesses. My ears are trained to detect false notes. Now then, I want to know, are you acting in good faith in this thing?"

"What do you mean, Mr. Mason?"

"Were you lying to me this morning?"

"Not at all. I was telling you the absolute truth."

"You didn't have anything fixed up with your father that you were to call me or . . . ?"

"Of *course* not, Mr. Mason. I was terribly concerned when I couldn't find Daddy—I know that things have been bothering him the last few days and my father told me that no matter what happened he didn't want to have anything to do with the police. I told you all that and it's the truth."

"Did he tell you why?"

"No, he just said that."

"Wasn't that rather unusual? In other words, wasn't that an unusual thing for him to say?"

"Yes, of course."

"And did you ask him why he said it?"

"Yes."

"And what did he say?"

"That's all tied in with some of the things I'm supposed to tell you. My father told me over the phone that I was to tell you everything while we were going out to get his brief case."

"All right," Mason said, "tell me everything."

"Well, Daddy makes investments of his own and he also acts as an investment counsel for other people and there are some pools of money that Daddy is empowered to invest—that is, Daddy's company. It's a corporation. He had it incorporated so that in case he should die suddenly in an accident of some sort or anything like that, the trust funds wouldn't be all mixed up with his estate."

"It's a corporation?"

"Yes. Gilman Associates Investment Pool."

"All right. What else?"

"Roger C. Calhoun is the business manager. My father is president."

"So what?" Mason asked.

"Well, of late Daddy has felt that Roger Calhoun is secretly trying to undermine him with some of the big investors, some of the people who put up money in the pools. You see, the corporation gets a percentage of the profits it makes. It's rather a small percentage but where the investments are big it amounts to quite a sum of money."

"Is your father in danger of losing control of the corporation?"

"No, no, nothing like that. He wouldn't lose control of the corporation. He has that all tied up. But he might lose the investors. That is, some of the big ones."

"And just who are the big ones?"

"Oh, heavens, I don't know all the names, but there are lots of big ones. There's a big lumberman up in the northern part of the state who lets Daddy handle nearly all of his investments and there's a widow down in the Imperial Valley who has more than half a million dollars Daddy is managing, and . . . well, there are just lots of people."

"Tell me a little more about Calhoun," Mason said.

"Well, he's young—that is, Daddy always calls him young. I think he's old—that is, he's much older than I am."

"How old is he?"

"Thirty-four, I think. But he's a very bright man. He makes a study of the market and . . . well, he's really bright."

Mason said abruptly, "Is your father counting calories?"

"In a way, yes, but what in the world—?"

Mason interrupted. "After a breakfast that was loaded with calories, he sent you back to the kitchen to cook up still another egg and some more sausage. . . . He did, didn't he?"

"Yes."

"Wasn't that rather a peculiar thing for him to do?"

"When you think about the calories, I guess it was."

"I'm just trying to get the picture straight," Mason said. "Now go on and tell me some more about Calhoun."

"Well, there were some agreements that had to be signed this morning. They were to be signed by the corporation. They were in Daddy's brief case and Mr. Calhoun is naturally very much upset because they weren't in the office and he didn't know where Daddy was."

"You went up to the office?"

"Yes."

"Why didn't you call on the telephone?"

"Oh, but I did call on the telephone and asked to have Daddy call me as soon as he came in. And Mr. Calhoun's secretary got on the line and said that I was to have Daddy call them just as soon as I got in touch with him. She wanted to know where he was and I told them . . . well, I played innocent, you know. I told them that, why, I had no idea if he wasn't at the office, that I had expected he would be there."

"You think they suspected anything?" Mason asked.

"Oh, no," she said, "I was careful not to let them know that there was anything out of the ordinary."

"Can you control your voice that well?"

"Oh, I think so. I was an actress in nearly all of the high-school plays and I did some work in college. They say I'm pretty darn good. I think probably I could have gone on professionally, only Daddy didn't want me to."

"You gave up your career for him?"

"It wasn't a career, Mr. Mason. It might have led to a career, I don't know. I guess every girl gets sort of stage-struck at one time or another if she has any natural aptitude, and they told me I had natural aptitude."

"Who told you?"

"Oh, everyone—the dramatic coaches, the . . . I have quite a scrapbook, Mr. Mason. I know you're altogether too busy to read it but I'm inordinately proud of it. I've got some really rave notices."

"Now, when you went to the office," Mason said, "why did you go there? Did you think someone was holding out on you over the telephone?"

"No. I wanted to talk with Tillie."

"That's your father's secretary?"

"Yes. Tillie Norman."

"Did you talk with her at that time?"

"No, she wasn't there. But she called up while I was there and told the switchboard operator that she wouldn't be in for about half an hour. She'd gone out on a coffee break and . . . well, she's Daddy's personal secretary and when he isn't there, there isn't much for her to do. So she did a little shopping and called the operator to find out if Daddy was in and to tell her she would be out for a while longer if Daddy wasn't there."

"And the operator told her you were there?"

"Yes."

"So then what happened?"

"Well, I told the operator as soon as I heard her mention Tillie's name that I wanted to speak with her—the operator knew I was looking for Tillie."

"So what did you do?"

"I told Tillie that I was anxious to get in touch with Daddy, and she said that she was, too; that he hadn't been in all day."

"So then what?"

"Well, Tillie asked me if anything was wrong and I was a little guarded. I told her no, nothing in particular, but that I was very anxious to get in touch with him."

"Then what happened?"

"Well, Tillie said that she would come right up to the office and if I'd wait there that she'd postpone her shopping trip and talk with me."

"So you waited?"

"Yes."

"And then what?"

"Well, Tillie came in and it was a good thing she did, for shortly afterward Daddy called and asked for Tillie to give her some confidential instructions and Tillie told him I was there; and Daddy said, 'Oh, good,' that he had been trying to reach me at the house and told Tillie to put me on the phone without letting anyone know he was calling."

"And then what?"

"Then Daddy told me that I was to go to your office, to get you and take you out to the house and give you his brief case, that you were to take the entire brief case and keep it in your office until he sent for it, that you were to take the agreements that were in the green Bristol-board folder out of the brief case and deliver those agreements to Mr. Calhoun.

"And Daddy told me that I was to talk with you going out and tell you absolutely everything that I knew about Daddy and the business and the background and about Mr. Calhoun and everything."

"Anything about your stepmother?" Mason asked.

"No, he didn't mention her name. Why? Is there anything about her?"

"I'm just trying to get your father's instructions," Mason said.

"Well, that's the whole story, Mr. Mason, as nearly as I

can tell you. Of course, there are lots of little things; if you'll ask me questions I'll try to answer them."

Mason said, "Well, let me think this over for a while."

He drove the automobile for some ten minutes in thoughtful silence. Then, just before they turned into Vauxman Avenue, Mason said, "Just a minute, I have one phone call to make."

The lawyer stopped the car in front of a telephone booth at the curb by a service station, got out and called his office. "Let me talk with Della, Gertie," he said when he had the office on the line.

Della Street's voice, cool and competent, came over the wire. "Yes, Chief, what is it? I have a notebook and pencil here."

Mason said, "It's rather simple, Della. Call up the office of Gilman Associates Investment Pool in the Piedmont Building. Ask to talk to Mr. Gilman personally. Tell him you're a widow with some funds to invest and you'd like to know something about their investment service."

"Then what?" Della Street asked.

"Gilman won't be in," Mason said, "so then ask if there's anyone who can tell you about making an appointment with Mr. Gilman. Ask if he has a secretary there."

"And then?" Della asked.

"You have a good ear for voices," Mason said. "When you get Mr. Gilman's secretary on the line, get her name, find out who is talking. If it's Miss Norman, give her a fictitious name and address, then go on and give her a song and dance about having some funds to invest and ask the secretary to describe the investment service."

"And then what?"

"Then tell her you'll think it over and hang up," Mason said.

"Just what is it you want to know?" she asked.

"I want to know what Gilman's secretary's voice sounds like over the telephone."

"So I can remember it again?"

"I think you'll remember it as soon as you hear it," Mason said. "Unless I'm chasing something up a blind alley, you'll find that the voice of Matilda Norman, Carter Gilman's private secretary, is the voice that assured us over the telephone she was Vera Martel, the detective."

"Oh-oh," Della Street said. "In other words, you've smoked something out?"

"There's a lot of smoke," Mason said. "I don't know where the fire is just yet and I want to be careful I don't get my fingers burned."

"How's your little friend Muriell?"

"Doing fine," Mason said. "How did she impress you?"

"She's sweet and . . . well, rather demure-looking."

"For your information," Mason said, "she's a very accomplished actress and she's had quite a bit of experience."

"All right," Della Street said, "I make this call. Then suppose the voice is that of Vera Martel, or rather the person who assured us she was Vera Martel; what do I do?"

"Just make an appointment," Mason said, "and hang up. And, incidentally, it might be well for you to disguise your voice a little, Della, because we may be having some further conversations with Matilda Norman."

"When do I do it?"

"Right away."

"And you'll be in touch with me later?"

"That's right. I'll telephone in for a report."

Mason hung up, returned to the car and smiled at Muriell. "Well, Muriell," he said, "I guess you'll have to forgive a rough, tough trial lawyer for being a little suspicious. After all, the events of the day have been just a little mysterious."

"I'll say they have," Muriell said, looking at him with wide brown eyes which radiated innocence, candor, and a certain concern.

"Now," Mason said, "if your father should come home tonight it would be advisable if you just talked with him normally and naturally and didn't tell him anything about my making that trip out to the house this morning or about you getting alarmed at his absence and calling me. Do you think you can do that?"

"Would it be for Daddy's best interests?"

"I'm quite certain it would be for his best interests," Mason said.

"In that case, I can do it."

"And get away with it?"

"Oh, sure," Muriell said. "If I don't want people to find out anything they don't find it out, that's all."

"All right," Mason said, suppressing a smile, "let's just keep our own counsel on that, Muriell. It may help."

"But what about that ten thousand dollars?"

Mason said, "No one except you and I knows when I got that. We'll go out to the workshop when we get to the house and . . . in fact, we'll drive right into the garage and go in the workshop from there. For your information, your father talked with me on the phone and told me to pick up the money that was on the floor in the workshop."

"Daddy didn't tell *me* anything about the money," Muriell said.

"Probably because he didn't have time," Mason said. "I think it's highly advisable that you let your father tell you just what he wants you to know and don't ask questions, and that you don't tell your father anything about our meeting this morning. Your father might not like the idea that you called me up just because he jumped up from the breakfast table."

"Yes, I've thought of that," she said. "Daddy might feel that I was getting a little . . . well, taking too much on myself."

"Exactly," Mason said and, turning into the driveway at the Gilman home, ran the car into the vacant garage and stopped.

"Where is everybody?" Mason asked.

"Well," she said, "Daddy has the sedan."

"And Nancy and Glamis?" Mason asked.

"Nancy and Glamis went to a meeting of a photographic club in the sports car and I took the club coupé uptown."

"I see," Mason said. "That accounts for all three cars and, because the sports car isn't here, I take it neither your stepmother nor Glamis has returned."

"That's right."

Mason said to Muriell, "I'll wait in the workshop while you run in and get the brief case. Incidentally, it might be a good idea to find out if anyone is home. I'd just as soon none of the others knew that I was out here unless . . . well, unless it becomes necessary. We won't try any subterfuge, but on the other hand, we won't advertise the fact that I'm here. I think that's the way your father would want it."

"I'm sure he'd want it that way," she said, opening the door to the darkroom. "Come right through the darkroom, Mr. Mason. You can wait in the workshop."

Mason followed Muriell across the darkroom into the workshop. Muriell smiled at him and said, "I'll get Daddy's brief case right away. I know exactly where it is. It's in the dining room. He had it with him ready to take to work this morning and then whatever happened when he left . . . Mr. Mason, why do you suppose he did leave in such a hurry?"

"Heavens, I don't know," Mason said. "Your father evidently has various business affairs. He has lots of irons in the fire. Something came up that demanded his attention, probably something he'd forgotten about."

She nodded and walked over to the door at the southeast corner of the workshop, said, "I'll be right back, Mr. Mason."

As soon as the door closed, Mason started making a swift but detailed survey of the workshop.

The broken chair was still lying on the floor. The pool of red enamel had partially dried. The room was warm and almost unnaturally quiet, filled with the smell of seasoned wood. A big fly droned in lazy circles.

A big blob of modeling clay was on the workbench. Mason regarded the clay carefully. There were fingerprints in the clay.

Mason moved back to the darkroom. He used a handkerchief so he would leave no fingerprints on the doorknob or the light switch and switched on the lights. He opened a few of the drawers. There were pictures of Carter Gilman, pictures of Muriell, pictures of an exceptionally beautiful blond young woman. Some were portrait enlargements, some were in bathing suits and one picture of the blonde was in a daring Bikini. It had been colored and Mason paused for a moment to look appreciatively at the girl's figure; then he replaced the photographs, looked in some of the negative files and then heard the clack of Muriell's heels on the hardtop as she returned to the workshop.

When she entered, Mason was innocently inspecting a partially finished jewel case.

"Your father does nice work," he said.

"Simply beautiful," she said. "He loves to work with wood and polish it. Isn't that a beautiful little jewel case? I think that's to be for me on my birthday."

"You have the brief case, I see," Mason said.

She handed it to him without a word.

"Now I'm to keep that in my office and simply deliver the papers that are in that green Bristol-board folder to Roger Calhoun?"

"That's right."

"I'm not to say anything about your father's business other than that he's consulted me?"

"That's right. Daddy just said you were to deliver the papers to Calhoun and tell him you were doing so at Daddy's request and the agreements were to be executed."

"That," Mason said, "might provoke some comment. Your father was scheduled to be at the office with these papers. Then a lawyer whose reputation is not exactly unknown comes walking into the office and says casually, 'I have the agreements Mr. Gilman was to bring into the office this morning.' "

Muriell said, "Well, I guess Daddy thought you were to use your own judgment."

"I'll use it," Mason said.

Suddenly Muriell cocked her head in a position indicating she was concentrating on listening.

"What is it?" Mason asked.

"A car turned into the driveway. Just a minute."

Muriell walked over to the Venetian blinds, separated two of the metallic leaves so that she could look through, and said, "Good heavens, it's Glamis coming home in a taxi!"

Mason regarded Muriell's distressed countenance. "You don't want her to know anything about this?"

"Heavens, no."

"Doesn't your father trust her?"

"I guess so, but . . . well, I just don't want her to know, that's all."

"So what do you do?" Mason asked.

"I try to divert her," she said. "But I don't think it can be done. If she ever sees your car in the garage she'll start looking around and, of course, if we aren't in the house she'll come out here. . . . It may be better for me to just go out and talk with her and . . . But if she sees me coming out of the workshop she'll wonder what I'm doing here, and if she finds you here . . . Oh, dear."

Mason studied Muriell thoughtfully. "You don't think she'll go right into the house and . . . ?"

"Let's hope so. She forgot to pay the cab. . . . That's just like her. . . . Now she's turning back to pay the cabby and . . . Oh-oh, she's seen your car! I'll go out and *try* to head her off. I doubt if I can do it. She's terribly curious.

If I can't stall her, don't tell her anything. Understand? Not anything."

Muriell opened the door of the workshop and walked, in a manner which she tried to make casual, down toward the taxicab.

Mason, parting the Venetian blinds to watch what was happening, saw the long-legged blonde whose picture he had seen in the darkroom smile vivaciously at Muriell and walk forward to put an arm around her.

Muriell exerted a gentle pressure toward the house and Glamis seemed to hold back slightly, asking questions.

Mason moved over to the telephone on the workbench, raised the instrument to his ear, caught the receiving tone and rapidly dialed the number of Paul Drake's office.

When he had the detective on the line, Mason said, "Paul, I'll have to give this to you quick and I can only give it to you once. I'm going to drive into my parking lot probably within the next twenty to thirty minutes. There'll be a young woman with me. I want you to have someone pick up that young woman's trail and tail her no matter where she goes."

"Have a heart, Perry," Drake said. "That's awfully short notice to get . . ."

"Do it yourself," Mason said, "if you can't get someone. I want it done. I think someone's giving me a runaround."

Mason hung up the phone and, again parting the slats on the Venetian blinds, saw that the two girls were still talking.

Mason dialed the number of his office. When Gertie answered the phone, he said, "Get me Della on the line quick, Gertie."

The lawyer heard the sound of voices outside. "Quick, Della," he said. "Did you get that call through?"

"I did," Della Street said, "and while her normal voice is much slower and not so high-pitched, the woman who is Carter Gilman's secretary is very definitely the same woman who called us and said she was Vera M. Martel."

Mason saw the doorknob of the door start to turn and abruptly dropped the telephone back into position and was idly inspecting one of the machines as Muriell Gilman said, "Mr. Mason, I want you to meet Glamis Barlow. Glamis, may I present Mr. Mason?"

Mason caught the full impact of the wide blue, curious yet audacious eyes.

Glamis came toward him with hand outstretched, her manner as seductive as an expert striptease artist walking out on the stage. "Why, how do you do?" she said. "Muriell told me she was here with a friend who was interested in woodworking."

Mason made no comment about Muriell's statement. He took Glamis' hand in his own, bowed and said, "It's a very great pleasure, Miss Barlow."

Glamis turned to Muriell. "Where's the other car, Muriell? I came to pick it up. I have to have it."

"Oh, good heavens, it's uptown," Muriell said. "I left it parked up there."

"You *left* it parked up there?"

"I accepted a ride out with Mr. Mason," she said.

Glamis frowned for a moment, then said, "How did you intend to get it?"

"Mr. Mason was going to drive me back uptown. I'll get it and bring it out here, Glamis."

"Then where are you going?"

"No place. I'm going to stay here. Mr. Mason is ready to leave and I'll go with him and—"

"There isn't time," Glamis said. "I'm sorry, Muriell, but I have to have the car right away. I'll ride up with Mr. Mason—just give me the parking ticket . . . that is, I will if Mr. Mason has no objections."

Muriell hesitated.

Mason bowed and said, "Perhaps you can both come with me."

"No," Glamis said imperiously. "Muriell wants to be home. If she got the car she'd just drive it back. I have places to go."

Muriell said reluctantly, "Well, I guess that's probably the only thing to do then. . . . You're ready to start, Mr. Mason?"

"Right away," Mason said.

"I saw your car in the garage," Glamis said. "I thought at first it was our other car, but then I realized it was a strange car. I asked Muriell who was here. . . . You're going right away, Mr. Mason?"

Muriell said, in a voice that was far from happy, "He'll *have* to leave right away. He has an important appointment."

"All right," Glamis said, "let's go."

She looked around the workshop, said, "Well, for heaven's sake, somebody's spilled something on the floor and look at that chair."

"It must have been tipped over," Muriell said.

"Heavens, Muriell, it's broken!"

"Well," Muriell said, "if you're in a hurry to get uptown, Glamis—"

"I am," Glamis interrupted. "And Mr. Mason is, also. Toodle-oo, Muriell. We'll be seeing you. Come on, Mr. Mason. I'm going to hurry you as much as I can because I really want the car, and Nancy took my sports car to go out on location with her photographic club, so I had to come home in a cab. I thought there'd at least be one car here."

"I'm sorry," Muriell said.

"What is there to be sorry about, honey? You're entitled to the car when you want it just as much as anyone. . . . I'm a little afraid I'm imposing on Mr. Mason, but . . . I *am* going to hurry you, Mr. Mason."

She inserted her hand in Mason's arm.

Mason picked up the brief case and started walking toward the car.

"Now," Glamis said, "if you're going to be polite and make this a social occasion, Mr. Mason, you'll escort me to the right-hand side of the car and open the door and I'll flash you a smile of thanks and try to reward you by giving you a quick glimpse of what I've been told is a very good-looking leg.

"If, on the other hand, this is strictly business . . ."

"Let's make it a social occasion, by all means," Mason said.

He waved to Muriell, walked around to the right-hand side of his car with Glamis and held the door open for her.

Glamis jumped in the car, smiled at him, then adjusted her skirt revealingly.

"Thank you, Mr. Mason."

"Not at all," the lawyer said. "The reward was ample."

Mason walked around to the other side of the car, tossed

the brief case in the back and climbed in behind the steering wheel.

Glamis, looking straight ahead, said, "You have a brief case that's exactly like Dad Gilman's."

"I guess all brief cases are pretty much alike," Mason said casually as he started the car and backed down the driveway.

Glamis said, "I'm afraid Muriell's been holding out on me, Mr. Mason. She hasn't told me anything about you. Have you known her long?"

"It depends on what you mean by long," Mason said. "Time is relative."

"Indeed it is. . . . So you're interested in woodworking?"

"Yes."

"Do you have a shop of your own?"

"I'm thinking of installing one."

"I'm quite sure Muriell has never mentioned you," Glamis said.

Mason said nothing.

"Somehow you're not the type that one associates with afternoons of dillydallying."

"I was neither dillying nor dallying," Mason said.

"My, you have a very adroit method of being evasive, Mr. Mason. Did it ever occur to you that I'm pumping you for information?"

"Are you?"

"Certainly I am. I want to know more about you. I want to know what makes you tick. Muriell isn't the playgirl type and you're . . . there's something purposeful about you, something substantial. You're not a playboy. You have some objective in life and you've come very close to achieving that objective—whatever you do, you're tops."

"Character analysis?" Mason asked.

She was studying him frankly as Mason drove through traffic.

"Character analysis," she said. "I like it. Sometimes I'm rather good at it. You're not a doctor . . . and you're not exactly the banker type. You're a professional man of some sort."

"Well," Mason said, "since you derive so much pleasure from speculating about my occupation and character it would be a shame to deprive you of that pleasure by telling you anything."

"You're being delightfully evasive, Mr. Mason," she said. And then added after a moment, "And it isn't going to do you a particle of good because when I get out I'm going to look at the license number on your automobile and then I'm going to trace the ownership and find out just who you are.

"You're some sort of a professional . . . Oh, good heavens, of course! You're a lawyer."

Mason said nothing.

"Mason. Mason," Glamis went on. "Well, bless my soul! You're *Perry* Mason!"

Mason simply kept on driving.

"And you don't give me the slightest credit for putting two and two together," Glamis went on. "You are acting very, very mysteriously, Mr. Mason. Now why in the world would *you* be out there, calling on Muriell of all people! And then when I catch you calling on Muriell, why should you be so evasive? . . . And that *is* Dad's brief case you're carrying, isn't it?"

Mason said, "As an attorney I would object to the question on the ground that it called for several answers."

"All different?"

"I don't think it's necessary to specify that in making an objection based on those grounds," Mason said.

Glamis inched up closer to him on the seat, put her left arm over the back of the seat so that the hand was touching Mason's right shoulder. She squirmed around, drawing her legs up in under her, then glanced down at her skirt and said, "I suppose I should be a little more modest —in the interest of safe driving," and pulled the skirt down.

For several seconds she studied the lawyer's granite-hard profile frankly and with a curiosity she made no attempt to conceal.

"Now, what in the world would *you* be doing out in Dad's workshop?" she asked.

"Perhaps," Mason said, "I gave you a true answer when I said I was interested in woodworking."

"And you didn't get in touch with Dad Gilman about it, you got in touch with Muriell. I'm *quite* certain Muriell hasn't known you more than twenty-four hours . . . if Muriell had known you, we'd have learned about it.

"Not that Muriell's a name-dropper, you understand, Mr. Mason, but she'd certainly have managed some way to have brought it into the conversation . . . 'As my friend, Mr. Perry Mason, the noted lawyer, said on occasion . . .' "

Glamis shook her head. "You're being very, very difficult, Mr. Mason. I see that I'm going to have to do some intensive research."

"Aren't you doing it now?"

"Heavens, no! I'm just hitting the high spots. I'm watching your face and noticing the very slight but very definite expression of irritation which comes around the corners of your eyes. Has anybody ever told you that you squint your eyes just the least little bit at the corners when you're being irritated, Mr. Mason?"

"I wasn't aware of it," Mason said.

They drove for a long while in silence, Glamis studying the lawyer.

Glamis laughed and said, "I didn't mean to irritate you, Mr. Mason. Now that I've smoked you out I think perhaps we should improve the opportunity to get acquainted personally and socially, and not let me pry into business matters which I'm quite certain you feel are no concern of mine.

"I wonder if you play golf . . . no, I don't suppose you have time. You're one of these tremendously busy people. You have all that drive and . . . well, there's an aura of success about you. Really, I'm rather proud of myself. You remember I said before I knew who you were that you'd be at the top of your profession."

Mason grinned. "I would say you were pretty good at character analysis and at flattery."

"I'm a splendid little prober," Glamis said. "I like to inquire into things. I like to listen to what people say and occasionally, when they make a slip, I look at them with an expression of most cherubic innocence.

"You know, it's wonderful to be young and able to look unsophisticated, Mr. Mason. I suppose a few years more and I won't be able to get away with it. . . . Still, you can't tell. If the expression of cherubic innocence has persisted so far in spite of my checkered career . . . Well, I guess we won't go into that. I'll be evasive myself."

"You make yourself sound delightfully mysterious," Mason said. "I know you're besieged by admirers, yet apparently you haven't said yes to anyone because there's no diamond on your left hand."

"Well, aren't *you* observing," she said. "For your information, Mr. Mason, the monosyllabic affirmative doesn't necessarily mean a diamond, in this day and age."

"That," Mason said, "has all the elements of being a cryptic wisecrack."

"How adroitly you've managed to shift the subject of conversation from you to me, Mr. Mason. And now I perceive by a slightly relaxed expression at the corner of your eyes that you're very much at ease, which means, I take it, that we're approaching your office building where you park your car. . . . I'd better look at the parking ticket Muriell gave me and see. . . . That's right, your parking lot is right ahead on the left. . . . That's the parking lot I usually use when I run into Dad Gilman's office to do errands. His office is in the Piedmont Building."

"My office is in this building right here," Mason said, as he turned into the parking lot.

"And, as a regular tenant, you have a duly assigned parking space, I see," she said, as Mason turned into the parking space.

"Exactly," Mason said.

She said, "If you'd walk around to the right-hand side of the car and let me out, Mr. Mason, I'd reward you again. But, after all, I'm in a terrific hurry and I know you want to get rid of me as soon as possible. It was nice seeing you and I hope I see you again.

" 'Bye, now."

She opened the door on the right-hand side of the car, jumped to the ground and hurried over to the parking attendant, holding out her parking ticket.

Mason sat for a moment in the car, then looked around for Paul Drake but was unable to spot him.

The lawyer retrieved the brief case from the car.

One of the parking attendants brought up the club coupé. Glamis Barlow flung open the door and jumped inside, slammed the door shut with one motion and swept the car into speed.

As she drove out of the parking lot Mason saw Paul Drake, driving his nondescript agency car, come from a stall on the other side and swing in behind her.

The lawyer tried to catch Drake's eye in order to flash him a signal but was unable to do so. After a moment he turned, walked to the sidewalk, then turned sharply to the left and walked to the Piedmont Building.

CHAPTER SIX

MASON ENTERED the offices of the Gilman Associates Investment Pool at precisely twenty-six minutes after five o'clock.

An exceptionally beautiful red-haired receptionist looked up from the switchboard and smiled as though she meant it.

"I'm Mr. Mason," the lawyer said. "I have an appointment with Mr. Calhoun."

"Oh, yes. Just a moment, Mr. Mason. He's waiting for you. In fact, we were all asked to wait."

She depressed a key, said, "Mr. Mason is here," then said, "You may go right on in, Mr. Mason, right down the passageway, and it's the second door on the right."

Mason glanced around the reception room, noting its deep carpet, comfortable chairs, and copies of some of the leading financial magazines on the table. As he walked past the door of an adjoining room he had a quick glimpse of batteries of filing cases and saw several secretarial desks equipped with typewriters and transcribing machines.

Down the corridor Mason walked past a door marked CARTER GILMAN and then beyond to a door marked ROGER C. CALHOUN.

Mason opened the door and entered another office in

which an attractive brunette who could well have posed for a calendar ad said, "Mr. Mason?"

The lawyer nodded.

"If you'll go right on to Mr. Calhoun's private office," she said, "he's expecting you."

Mason went through the door she indicated and entered an office where a small-boned, wiry man in the early thirties sat in a big chair behind a massive desk.

The man got up, walked around the desk and said, "Mr. Mason, I'm pleased to meet you."

Long, bony fingers gripped the lawyer's hand.

"Please be seated, Mr. Mason."

Calhoun indicated a comfortable chair, then walked around to the other side of the desk, seated himself in the armchair, propped his elbows on the arm of the chair, extended long, tapering fingers, touched the tips of the fingers of each hand together and assumed his most impressive manner.

Mason said, "I am an attorney at law, Mr. Calhoun, and—"

"Yes, yes, I know all about you, Mr. Mason."

Mason bowed his head. "And I am here," he said, "on rather a peculiar matter. I have been asked to deliver to you some contracts which I believe Mr. Gilman has been working on. I think it is only fair to state that I am somewhat in the nature of a common carrier in the matter. I am delivering contracts which I haven't read and about which I know nothing except I was instructed to deliver them and to instruct you that they were to be executed."

Calhoun sat forward in the chair, parted his hands and said eagerly, "Yes, yes, Mr. Mason, I've been waiting for those contracts all day. A very important business deal is pending and . . . can you tell me where Mr. Gilman is?"

"I'm afraid I can't at the moment," Mason said, with his voice indicating courteous surprise. "He hasn't been in touch with you?"

"He has not," Calhoun said, snapping the words out. "It is most unusual. May I see the contracts, please?"

Mason opened the brief case, pulled out the green Bristol-board jacket on which had been scribbled the notation to call Perry Mason in the event of an emergency and giving Mason's telephone number.

The lawyer carefully extracted the blue-backed contracts.

"It's all right," Calhoun said impatiently, his eyes on the inked notation. "Just give me the entire folder, Mr. Mason."

The lawyer said evenly, "My instructions were to deliver the contracts."

He handed four contracts over to Calhoun.

Calhoun looked through the contracts to make sure they were all copies of the same instrument, then he turned the pages of the instrument with a quick motion of his long forefinger and thumb. He did this in a practiced manner as though he had long been accustomed to turning pages or perhaps counting money.

When he had finished he looked up with grave dignity and said, "Thank you very much, Mr. Mason."

There was something about the man's slender, youthful appearance that made his attempt to impress visitors with the massive furniture of his office, the grave dignity of his manner, seem slightly incongruous.

Mason said, "Since I am acting in an unusual capacity here and in connection with a situation which is somewhat unusual, I would like to have a receipt showing that I have delivered the contracts and showing the time, if you please."

Calhoun hesitated a moment, then pressed a button.

A moment later his secretary stood in the doorway.

"Will you bring your notebook, Miss Colfax?" he asked.

The secretary smiled. "I have it here, Mr. Calhoun."

She moved easily into the room, pulled up a small secretarial chair, crossed her knees, giving a generous display of remarkably well-proportioned legs, and poised her notebook on the crossed knee.

"You will write the date, which is the thirteenth," Roger Calhoun said in the meticulous voice of a schoolteacher giving instructions to pupils. "You will mark the exact time, which at the moment of this delivery was five thirty-two. You will make the receipt to Perry Mason, an attorney at law, and you will note in the receipt that Mr. Mason has delivered to me the original and three copies of a contract covering the proposed purchase by the corporation of all rights in the Barclay Mining Syndicate. You will note that these contracts are delivered for signature by Mr. Mason as attorney for Carter Gilman, who has approved the deal in its present form."

"Just a minute," Mason interrupted. "I think we had better leave off that about approving the deal. My instructions were only to deliver the contracts and state they were to be executed."

"But that's the sole idea in having the contracts executed," Calhoun said. "If Gilman doesn't approve the entire deal he wouldn't have said to execute the contract."

"I am interested in your statement to that effect," Mason said, "but the fact remains that I know nothing whatever about whether Mr. Gilman approves the entire deal."

Calhoun hesitated a moment, then said, "I think, in order to protect myself, Miss Colfax, I will ask you to type the receipt as I dictated it."

"All right," Mason said. "In order to protect myself, I'll strike out the phrase about Gilman's approval of the entire deal at the time the receipt is handed to me."

"I fail to see that the point is of such devastating importance, Mr. Mason," Calhoun said coldly.

"The matter is of importance as far as I'm concerned," Mason said. "There's nothing devastating about it. That's your adjective. I don't know what's important to you. I know what's important to me."

Calhoun took a deep breath, said, "Very well, Miss Colfax, you may strike out the phrase about Gilman's approval and type the receipt, please. Make it in triplicate."

"Yes, Mr. Calhoun," she said.

She got to her feet and left the room.

Calhoun looked at his watch and said, "While we are waiting, I would like to discuss some matters which pertain to your client."

"I haven't authority to discuss anything," Mason said. "My sole authorization was to deliver papers."

"There is no reason why you can't listen."

Mason said, "I'll listen to anything."

Calhoun once more assumed what apparently was his favorite pose of putting his fingertips together, said, "This is a business dealing with investments. In order to carry on the business it needs a great deal of skill in appraising the market trends and it, of course, requires that our clients have the utmost confidence in the integrity of the executive personnel."

Calhoun paused as though expecting some sign of agreement, but Mason didn't so much as nod his head.

Calhoun said, "I don't know how much you know about the history of your client, Mr. Mason, or about his background. I take it that you must know something."

As Mason remained silent, Calhoun went on, evidently somewhat nettled. "There are certain things in the background of Mr. Gilman which I hadn't discovered until recently. Mr. Gilman was married and has one child by that marriage, a very charming young woman, Muriell, who is now, I believe, about twenty years of age.

"His wife died and about five years ago Gilman married his second wife, Nancy. She had been married to Steven A. Barlow, who is at present living in Las Vegas, Nevada and was divorced from him. There is one child, presumably a child of that marriage, named Glamis, who is also a young woman of about twenty years of age.

"I had always supposed that Glamis was the child of the marriage between Nancy and Steven A. Barlow, but recently it has been called to my attention that Glamis is twenty years of age, yet the Barlow marriage was solemnized nineteen years ago. There are some other rather peculiar factors in the background of Glamis. I understand a detective has recently been looking up all these facts.

"Nancy Gilman is an unconventional, Bohemian type. If there should be any scandal involving the daughter it could have serious repercussions as far as this business is concerned."

Calhoun stopped speaking and looked accusingly at Mason, as though in some way Mason were responsible for the taint of illegitimacy.

Mason said, "If it's a fair question, how did you get your information about Glamis and about her illegitimacy?"

"The information came to me from a source which I consider authentic," Calhoun said.

"All right," Mason told him, "you've made a statement. I've listened."

Calhoun moved to the office intercom, depressed a key and said, "Miss Colfax, are the receipts ready?"

The musical voice of the secretary said, "They are ready, Mr. Calhoun. I was waiting to see if you wished them brought in."

"Bring them in," Calhoun said.

The door opened and Miss Colfax entered the office and handed the three receipts to Calhoun.

Calhoun read the receipts, signed all three of them, handed one to Mason and said, "That's all, Miss Colfax."

She turned and left the office. There was something in the way in which she walked which indicated she was conscious of the fact both men were watching her back as she left the room and that she was not at all displeased.

Mason said, "Well, I guess that covers everything I have to do here."

"I am very anxious to see Mr. Gilman," Calhoun said.

"How much longer will you be here?" Mason asked.

"At least for another hour."

"How about Mr. Gilman's secretary?" Mason asked casually. "Is she in the office? I would like to speak to her."

Calhoun depressed a key, said, "Miss Colfax, will you find out if Miss Matilda Norman is in Mr. Gilman's office?"

He sat waiting by the interoffice communication unit until the voice of the secretary said, "Miss Norman has left for the night, Mr. Calhoun."

Calhoun said very formally, "Thank you, Miss Colfax," and switched off the intercom. "It is long past closing time. I had some of the employees work overtime."

Mason said, "Thank you, and good night."

"Good night, Mr. Mason," Calhoun said.

Mason left the private office, walked across the outer office, paused in the doorway and looked back at the gorgeous brunette. "Good night, Miss Colfax."

Her eyes softened into an amused smile. "Good night, Mr. Mason," she said, and her right eye closed in a deliberate wink.

The lawyer walked down the street to his own office building and stopped in Paul Drake's office.

"Any news from Paul?" he asked the girl at the switchboard.

She shook her head. "He went out on a job for you, Mr. Mason, right after you phoned and he hasn't been back. He couldn't get an operative who was available."

"Okay," Mason said. "Tell him I want to see him when he comes in."

The lawyer walked down to his private office, latchkeyed the door and said to Della Street, "Well, here's Carter Gilman's brief case. Let's look through it and see what's in it. I delivered some contracts and here's the cardboard jacket they were in, a jacket that has the notation on it Muriell told me about. Let's see what else is in the brief case."

They looked through it together and found only half a dozen timetables of the various airlines leaving Los Angeles, plus a notation giving the address: Steven A. Barlow, 5981 Virginia City Avenue, Las Vegas, Nevada.

"Well?" Della Street asked.

"For your information," Mason said, "I have recently been associating with some very, very beautiful women."

"Does the adventure bear repetition or verbal description?" Della Street asked.

Mason said, "In the first place, I have had a delightful visit with our Miss Muriell Gilman, a young woman who has considerable ability as an actress and is somewhat proud of the manner in which she can use an air of childish innocence to cover up a background of thought which she feels is quite sophisticated.

"Then there is a curvaceous character by the name of Glamis Barlow who is blond, blue-eyed, very seductive and feels that gentlemen who assist her into automobiles should be given a generous glimpse of what she herself describes as a very good-looking leg."

"You fascinate me," Della Street said. "You mean I have been neglecting my feminine prerogatives by jumping casually into cars instead of waiting for men to assist me?"

Mason said, "I always felt that women liked to know the latest approach so that they could be in style."

"Your hint is appreciated. There have been others?"

"Oh, many others," Mason said. "There is a red-headed receptionist in the office of the Gilman company that has probably provoked as many whistles as any railroad crossing in the country. Then there is a young woman named Colfax who somehow manages to take dictation in a manner as suggestive as the motions of a striptease artist in taking off a pair of long-sleeved gloves—in other words, she has the ability to invest a thoroughly conventional action with an unconventional atmosphere, if you get what I mean."

"I get what you mean," Della Street said. "In the meantime, I am interested in knowing more about the personality of Mr. Gilman's private secretary, because there is no doubt on earth that she is the woman who telephoned and stated that she was Vera Martel, delivered the mysterious message about the fingerprints and gave us the number where Mr. Gilman could be reached. For your further information, Mr. Mason, that number was the number of a public pay-station telephone. It is in a booth about four blocks from the building where Mr. Gilman has his office."

Mason said, "Miss Matilda Norman, the secretary in question, had left for the night. She is reported to be somewhere in the fifties and is built along the lines of a string bean."

"These other women, I take it," Della Street said, "were not built along the lines of string beans."

"Definitely not," Mason said. "They were built like a mountain highway in Mexico. In other words, they were full of curves."

"And hard-surfaced?" Della Street asked.

"Well," Mason said, "they had an appearance which would indicate that all operations would be close to the maximum speed."

"*You* didn't exceed the limit, I take it."

"Oh, definitely not," Mason said. "I met a very pompous young man who takes himself very, very seriously indeed; a man who is saturated with college economics, with the analsyis of financial trends, who would exude stock-market quotations as a wrestler would exude perspiration."

"My, but we're getting flowery," Della Street said.

"That," Mason told her, "is due entirely to the atmosphere of the office I have just visited. If you have any surplus funds that you wish to invest I would recommend the Gilman company. It is painfully conscious of the fact that its stability depends upon keeping the reputations of the executive personnel free from the slightest taint.

"And, for your further information, Mr. Calhoun has recently made the startling discovery that Glamis Barlow, the long-legged blonde with the seductive habits, was born a year too soon to be the legitimate offspring of the Barlow marriage."

"Dear, dear," Della Street said. "I'm surprised your Mr. Calhoun could bear up under such a horrible example of moral depravity.

"Good Lord, Chief, I'm catching the pompous mood myself. Suppose *I* should start exuding stock-market quotations?"

"No," Mason said. "Your way of fitting into the picture would be to practice walking from the office the way Miss Colfax does."

"And how's that?"

"I can't describe the means, only the general effect. It is like a snake walking on its tail while holding its head rigidly motionless."

Suddenly the lawyer lost his bantering manner and said, "To hell with it, Della, what do you say we go out and get dinner? We'll leave word for Paul where we are. I gave him a tailing job, thinking he was going to tail Muriell, because I wanted to find out whether she went directly to her father after I dropped her at her car. However, Glamis took over the parking ticket from Muriell and now Paul Drake is shadowing Glamis on an expedition which may be rather unprofitable—at least as far as advancing the case is concerned."

Mason and Della Street walked down the hall and stopped in at Paul Drake's office, which was by the elevators.

Mason said to the girl at the switchboard, "There is no use our sitting around the office waiting for Paul to report. Della and I are going down to the Green Mill. We're going to have a couple of cocktails and some of their corn fritos, then we're going next door to the Steak Mart and we're going to have filet mignon with baked potato, garlic toast, French fried onions, apple pie à la mode and—"

"Don't, Mr. Mason, please," the receptionist begged. "I'm trying to take off two pounds and my stomach thinks all lines of communication have been severed."

"Well, we'll be back after a while," Mason said. "When Paul telephones in a report, tell him where we are and he can either call us there or come on down and join us."

Mason and Della Street went down to the Green Mill, sat in a booth in the dim light, relaxed in air-conditioned comfort and had two leisurely cocktails interspersed with fritos and potato chips.

"I think," Mason told Della Street, "you'd better call the Gilman residence and ask for Muriell. I think a woman's voice would attract less attention than a man's voice. When you get Muriell on the phone, ask her if she can talk and . . . well, I'll talk with her myself."

Mason signed the check for the cocktails, they moved over to the phone booth and Della Street called Gilman's residence and asked for Muriell. After a moment she said, "Just a minute, Miss Gilman. Mr. Mason wants to talk."

Mason said, "Hello, Muriell. How's everything coming? Is your dad home?"

"Oh, hello," Muriell said, without mentioning Mason's name. "It's nice to hear from you. Do you know anything new?"

"I carried out instructions," Mason said. "The contracts were delivered. I got a receipt from Roger Calhoun."

"Oh, that's fine!"

"Has your father come home yet?"

"No. He telephoned Nancy that he was going to be away, he wouldn't be back tonight. He said, however, that he'd be in the office tomorrow. He's getting in about nine o'clock in the morning, I believe."

"Where is he?" Mason asked.

"He had to go to Las Vegas, Nevada, on business."

"I see. Is Glamis there?"

"No, she isn't. She telephoned she wouldn't be in until quite late. With Glamis that means quite early."

"Well, that's fine," Mason said. "I just wanted you to know that the contracts had all been delivered. I guess we'll hear from your father tomorrow. Good night, Muriell."

Mason hung up the phone and grinned at Della Street. "Now this," he said, "is good. We gave Paul Drake an assignment to follow Glamis and evidently Glamis is out on quite a party. She phoned she wouldn't be home—probably until the small hours. That gives us a good guess as to why we haven't heard from Paul Drake."

"How utterly charming," Della Street said. "And it turned out Glamis was the wrong girl—you wanted him to shadow Muriell?"

"I did want him to shadow Muriell," Mason said, "but

as events are turning out now I think it's a good thing he's shadowing Glamis. We have duplicate daughters, each of whom seems to be steeped in mystery.

"Now, let us go get some food and intersperse the eating with a few dances and some leisurely discussion of clients, of duplicate daughters and second marriages, of mysterious showers of hundred-dollar bills and the unmistakable charm of the unexpected."

Hours later, back in Drake's office, the receptionist looked at them and smiled. "You fairly reek of being well fed," she said. "To a girl that's on a diet of cottage cheese, preserved pears and buttermilk, that's almost a crime. I haven't heard—" She broke off as a light flashed on the switchboard. She put in a plug, said, "Drake Detective Agency . . . yes . . . yes, he's right here, Mr. Drake. I'll put him on.

"Paul Drake calling from Las Vegas, Nevada," she said.

Mason grinned. "Where's a phone?"

"Go right down to Mr. Drake's private office. I'll put him on there."

Mason and Della Street hurried down the narrow passageway to Drake's private office. Mason picked up the phone, winked at Della Street and said, "Perry Mason, Paul. What the heck are *you* doing in Las Vegas?"

"Well, you told me to follow this party," Drake said, "and this is where I wound up."

"Why didn't you telephone me for a clearance to see if—?"

"There wasn't time," Drake said. "She drove directly to the airport and parked the car. I followed her into the plane office. There was a plane leaving for Las Vegas within ten minutes. She got a ticket and I managed to get a ticket. I tried to keep away from her, but as it turned out the only other vacant seat was right across the aisle from her."

"Did she look you over?"

"She did indeed," Drake said. "I think she may have become a little suspicious. I'll tell you what happened."

"What?"

"When she got to Las Vegas she took a taxicab into town. I naturally got another cab to follow the one she was in. She went to one of the big casinos, started playing the slot machines like mad, then she gave me the slip."

"How come?"

"After twenty or thirty minutes," Drake said, "a taxicab pulled up in front of the place and the fare got out. The time was nine eleven. This girl suddenly made a bolt for the door, shot into the cab, said something to the driver and the cab sped out into the street, leaving me standing there with the memory of a good look at a beautiful pair of gams and the nearest cab half a block away.

"By the time I'd sprinted up to that cab and got it started we were blocked by a traffic signal and after that we were licked. I never got a smell of the other cab. I went back to the casino to try and locate the cab she used, but it hasn't shown up yet. So I thought I'd phone in a report. I lost her trail at nine twelve."

Mason said, "Here's a tip for you, Paul. There's a Steve Barlow in Las Vegas. I don't know what he does. He lives at 5981 Virginia City Avenue. Go out and case his place. You may find your blonde there, talking with him. If you do, just catch the next plane back to Los Angeles."

"And if I don't find her?"

"Give the place a general once-over," Mason said, "but

it's not important enough to stay overnight. See if you can pick up her trail. If she's there, your job is finished. If she isn't, don't bother too much. I'll see you in the morning."

"Okay," Drake said. "I'll be seeing you.

Mason hung up the telephone, said to Della Street, "Well, I guess that about winds it up for the day, Della."

CHAPTER SEVEN

IT WAS ten thirty in the morning when Paul Drake tapped his code knock on the door of Mason's private office.

Della Street let him in.

"Hi, beautiful," Paul said.

"How was the gambling?" Della Street asked. "And did you put it on the expense account?"

"Believe it or not," Drake said, "I won nearly five hundred dollars."

"No wonder you were late getting in this morning," Mason said. "I presume you stayed all night, took the early-morning plane and—"

"I did nothing of the sort," Paul Drake said. "Actually, I finished my gambling by a little after midnight, took the next plane in, then came up to the office to get the information from my various operatives correlated so I could submit an intelligent report.

"Incidentally, Perry, you called the turn all right on this blond babe you had me shadowing. She was visiting with Steven A. Barlow at 5981 Virginia City Avenue. I went out there and staked out for about an hour, then she came out of the house, called a taxi and went uptown."

"Did you tail along?"

"Actually, I didn't, Perry. I had rented a car and the

only place that I could park it where I could be sure of watching the front door of the house was in a position where I had to park with my car pointed away from town.

"While I was sitting there trying to find some good excuse for ringing the doorbell so I could see who came to the door without betraying myself, a taxicab swung around the corner, pulled up in front of the house and stopped. The front door opened. A man whom I suppose was Steven Barlow and this blonde I'd been shadowing came out on the porch. She kissed him good-by, hurried down and jumped in the cab and the cab took off uptown. The man stood in the doorway watching the cab until it was out of sight. If I had tried to make a U-turn and follow, it would have been a dead giveaway, and since you had told me that if she was visiting Steven Barlow to forget about it, I just decided to call it a day."

Mason nodded. "That's right. I'm glad you played it that way."

"But," Drake said, "I ran into her again about eleven o'clock. She was in one of the casinos playing roulette and having quite a run of luck. By that time she'd changed into a clinging cocktail gown."

"Did she spot you this time?" Mason asked.

"Not me," Drake said. "I kept at the other end of the casino, but I was where I could watch her out of the corner of my eye. I was at one of the crap tables, and, believe me, Perry, that's the way to win money."

"What is?"

"Standing and watching somebody. I stood in one position and just kept putting a stack of five silver dollars down and leaving them there until somebody would either rake them in or pay me money. After a while I bought chips and got to putting down twenty-dollar chips."

"Did anyone notice you were spotting the girl?"

"No one. But here's a laugh for you. Some of them thought I had a new system of playing craps by putting the money down without looking at the table and keeping my head turned, so pretty quick half of the people at the table were putting money down and keeping their heads turned away."

"Did it work for them?"

"Not worth a damn," Drake said. "I had all the luck at the table."

"But you think this girl had spotted you when she ran out and jumped in the cab?"

"I'm hanged if I know, Perry. She's the impulsive sort. She does everything on impulse. Now, last night when she got in that car and drove out of the parking lot I'm satisfied she had some other destination in mind. But about the time she got to Hollywood she suddenly had a different idea. She took a look at her wristwatch, spun the car into a turn on La Brea and started crowding traffic for all she was worth."

"Then you think her visit to Barlow was impromptu?"

Drake nodded. "Who was this babe, by the way, Perry?"

"Glamis Barlow. She's the daughter of—"

"Glamis!" Drake exclaimed. "Good heavens! Why didn't I realize it!"

"You have something on her?" Mason asked.

"Lots of things," Drake said. "I got this story from a source I can trust. It's been kept hushed up and not a breath of it got in the papers. But here's what happened—I should have taken a tumble when you told me to look up Steven A. Barlow in Las Vegas, but, of course, I didn't have this information at that time. It was lying on my desk here.

"Here's the story and it's one for the book: Nancy Adair was living in Greenwich Village in New York as a free-lance, uninhibited artist. She was taking a fling at that time at story writing as well as her art work. I guess her stories weren't bad at that. She was making a living.

"If you knew Greenwich Village at that time, you get the atmosphere. There was a young writer there, John Yerman Hassell, who was going to write the great American novel and was going to take the world apart. He was about seven or eight years older than Nancy. He was from Texas, had an uncle down there who died and left him acres of dust.

"Hassell and Nancy had an affair and Nancy became pregnant. She wanted Hassell to marry her and Hassell, I guess, was a little disagreeable about the whole situation. He pointed out to her that they were both emancipated, that they didn't believe in the conventions, that they were living their own lives, that they were geniuses, that, as such, they must be uninhibited, that Nancy had got herself into trouble and she could damn well get herself out of trouble."

"So what happened?"

"Nancy stuck around for about three months, then suddenly disappeared. And I mean she disappeared completely. She disappeared so completely that later on, when oil was developed on Hassell's property and he became a multimillionaire, when he had a change of heart and looked back on his affair with Nancy and realized that he really was in love with her, when he spent thousands of dollars on private detectives, he couldn't even get a trace of her. He put ads in the papers, did everything he could."

"Why the sudden change of heart?" Mason asked.

"I guess he'd learned more about women in the meantime," Drake said. "This Nancy is quite a character."

"So I've heard," Mason said.

"Well, to get back to the story," Drake said, "Nancy took steps to cover up. She changed her name, came to Los Angeles, had her child and a few weeks later met Steve Barlow.

"Barlow lived in San Francisco. He was rather unconventional himself and Nancy appealed to him. They were married and moved up north someplace. Barlow was speculating in real estate and he turned a nice deal up there and he and Nancy went to live in Portland, Oregon. He made another deal in some timberland there and they moved to Bend, Oregon. After a while they split up. Later on, Nancy married Gilman."

"How much of all this does Glamis know?" Mason asked.

"Not a bit of it," Drake said. "She thinks Steve Barlow is her real father and I guess Steve is tremendously attached to her. I didn't know he was living in Las Vegas or I'd have put two and two together. The last I heard of him he was in Bend, Oregon, but I do know that when they split up the divorce decree provided that Steve Barlow had the right to visit his daughter at all reasonable and seasonable times."

"Now, what about Hassell?" Mason asked.

"Six years ago Hassell died. He had never married. He left an estate running into big money and he left a cool three million after all taxes to any person who could prove he or she was the child that had been born out of wedlock to Nancy Adair, formerly of New York, and he fixed the approximate date of birth and tied it all up in the will with legal strings.

"Nancy had washed her hands of him when he had refused to stand by her when she got into trouble, but the papers were full of the strange provision in the will, so Nancy quietly went to the heirs and told them she was going to file a claim on behalf of Glamis.

"The heirs were a brother and sister, and there was lots of money in the estate. They told Nancy to hold off while they made a check. And I guess they really made a check. That's where I got my information. One of the investigators who was employed by the brother and sister told my operative the whole story a couple of years ago, and when my operative found I wanted a check on Nancy Gilman he remembered about it and went back and got the details.

"It seems that Nancy was able to show rent receipts showing she'd been living at the apartment in Greenwich Village which was mentioned in Hassell's will. She couldn't prove anything by a birth certificate because she'd used an assumed name when she had the child, but there was something a lot better than that. It seems that there was such a marked family resemblance that as soon as the brother and sister saw Glamis they decided she was it. They offered a million and a half for settlement and finally made a settlement of around two million bucks after all taxes had been paid. There was a proviso in the settlement that the matter should be kept secret so that Glamis wouldn't be given the stigma of being illegitimate. By that time, Glamis was growing up and Nancy wanted her to have all the breaks."

"That was after she married Gilman?" Mason asked.

"About a year before."

"Where does Glamis think the money came from if she doesn't know anything about the will and the settlement?" Mason asked.

"That I can't tell you. Nancy has covered up in some way, but that's generally the story."

Mason got up and started pacing the floor. "Well," he said, "that's the kernel of the nut."

"What is?"

"The blackmail," Drake said. "This Vera Martel has found out about it in some way and she's putting the heat on Nancy, or perhaps on Glamis, or perhaps on both of them."

The phone rang.

Della Street picked it up, said, "It's for you, Paul."

Drake scooped up the instrument, said, "Hello, I'm coming right back to the office. If it's anything that'll wait . . . What! . . . You're sure? . . . Okay, give me the details."

Drake stood listening at the telephone for a good three minutes, then he said, "Okay. Get men on the job. Find out everything you can. . . . That's right, give it the works. Don't spare any expense."

Drake hung up the telephone. Mason, grinning, said, "You're spending a lot of someone's money, Paul. I'd hate to be the client in that case."

Drake looked at him with troubled eyes. "You are," he said. "Police found the body of Vera Martel early this morning. She was in her automobile and the automobile had apparently gone out of control and gone over a mountain grade back up around Mulholland Drive somewhere.

"However, there are lots of things about the case that are suspicious. The cops started with the idea that the car had been deliberately driven off the road at a place where there was an almost perpendicular drop of more than a hundred feet. Then they got the body to the coroner's office and a couple of hours ago the coroner gave them the information that it was murder, that there was a broken hyoid bone, distinctive petechial hemorrhagic spots and that Vera Martel had been quite dead when the automobile was pushed over the cliff.

"So the police started doing some high-class detective work and they found sawdust ground into Vera's skirt and some sawdust in the inside of her shoes. It wasn't the ordinary kind of sawdust but the sort that comes from a workshop where someone deals in rare woods—the kind one has as a hobby."

"How long has she been dead?" Mason asked.

"The best guess is that she died somewhere between seven o'clock yesterday morning and noon. If the police hadn't found the body when they did—in other words, if the body had remained there for a couple of days longer—police would have had great difficulty in fixing the time of death. The body was discovered because of good work on the part of a highway patrol who happened to notice peculiar automobile tracks in the dirt shoulder of the road. If it hadn't been for that, the body could have been there for days or weeks, because it was impossible to see the car unless someone got off the road and climbed partway down the mountain. The car had rolled over into a clump of scrub oak and was almost completely concealed."

Mason said, "How long have the police been working on this thing, Paul?"

"Since a little after daylight. They didn't let the news leak out for a while and now they're really closing a lot of loose ends. They—"

The telephone from the outer office rang. Della Street picked up the instrument and said, "Yes, Gertie." And then she said to Mason, "It's Muriell Gilman. She's on the line and Gertie says she's all but hysterical. She wants to talk with you right away."

"Put her on," Mason said, "I'll talk with her."

The lawyer picked up the telephone, said to Della Street, "You stay on the line, too, Della."

Della nodded, said, "Put her on, Gertie."

Mason heard a click and said, "Hello, Muriell. This is Mr. Mason."

"Oh, Mr. Mason, the most terrible thing has happened," Muriell said.

"All right," Mason said. "Now, keep calm and tell me in as few words as possible what it is. We may not have much time."

"The police were out here with a search warrant, Mr. Mason."

"All right," Mason said. "Who was home at the time?"

"All three of us. Nancy was asleep. Glamis got home in the small hours this morning and she was asleep. But I was up."

"All right," Mason said. "The police served the warrant on you?"

"Yes. They asked me who was in charge here and I said I guessed I was and they said they wanted to look in Daddy's woodworking shop."

"Did they?"

"Yes."

"What did they do?"

"They had a man who had some sort of a vacuum-sweeping attachment and he got sawdust off the floor and they looked at the broken chair and at the upset paint and they took some powder and dusted the can of enamel and there were fingerprints on it and they photographed those, and then they told me I had better wait outside but not to go near a phone."

"How long ago was that?"

"It must have been half or three quarters of an hour."

"Then what?"

"Then they left and . . . well, they were very nice, but they wouldn't answer questions. I kept asking them if there was some trouble, but they said they couldn't answer questions, that their job was to get information and not give it out."

"All right," Mason said. "Where's your father?"

"He's been in Las Vegas. He was supposed to be back on an early-morning plane and was supposed to be at the office at nine o'clock, but Mr. Calhoun called at nine thirty and said Daddy hadn't shown up and asked if I knew where he was."

"What did you tell Calhoun?"

"Mr. Mason, I—I lied to him."

"What did you tell him?"

"I told him I didn't know where Daddy was at the moment. I left the impression Daddy had been here for breakfast."

"Did he ask if your father had been home last night?"

"No, he didn't ask that specifically. He asked me if Daddy had intended to be at the office this morning and I told him I was quite sure he was going to be there."

"All right," Mason said. "Now, the police left there how long ago?"

"About ten minutes ago."

"Why didn't you call me sooner?"

"I was just completely flabbergasted. I didn't know what to do. I felt as though my knees had turned to rubber. I didn't know whether to tell Glamis and Nancy or what to do."

"What did you do?"

"I haven't wakened either Nancy or Glamis."

Mason said, "I want to talk with Nancy and I want to talk with Glamis. It's probably better for me to go out there than to have you come in here. I—"

The door from the outer office opened and Lt. Tragg of Homicide, his distinctive black hat tilted somewhat to the back of his head, entered the room. A plain-clothes officer followed behind him.

"Well, well, good morning, folks," he said. "I see you're busy as usual here."

Mason said in a sufficiently loud voice so Muriell would have no difficulty hearing him, "Well, well! What brings the Lieutenant of Homicide to my office this morning, and why don't you ask to be announced? It's only a trifling formality but it indicates a certain consideration for the conventions."

"I've repeatedly told you, the taxpayers don't pay me

to be considerate of conventions," Lt. Tragg said. "I could waste a lot of the taxpayers' time waiting in people's outer offices. And then again, Perry, it would give people an opportunity to prepare for my visit. They could perhaps remove evidence or think things over a little bit, or sometimes they might even slip out of the side exit door and then their secretary would be able to say quite truthfully that the man I wanted to see was gone and she didn't know just where he could be located.

"I think I've got my singulars and plurals all mixed up there somehow, Mason, but I'm quite certain you get the idea. Now, go right ahead with your telephone conversation."

"I had just about completed my telephone conversation," Mason said. And then said into the telephone, "Was there anything else?"

Muriell said, "Oh, Mr. Mason, something terrible has happened. I know it has. I—"

Mason interrupted to say, "Well, that's most interesting. Now, a matter has come up which is going to keep me occupied for some little while. I'll probably have to call you back when I can get at the documents in the case. As it happens, a Homicide inspector has appeared at the office. They are a little troublesome at times because they always insist on their affairs being given the right-of-way. It may take me a little while to find out what this is all about.

"I'll be calling you back as soon as I have a reasonable opportunity, but I'll have to investigate those documents first. Now, those matters which I suggested you keep in confidence are, I take it, still confidential. You haven't told anyone about them?"

"You mean about the—?"

"About *any* of them," Mason interrupted firmly.

"No, Mr. Mason, they didn't ask too many questions. They were asking about Daddy and I told them that he was in Las Vegas and was due in on the early-morning plane."

"Well, I'll be calling you back," Mason said. "Just hang around the telephone so you don't miss my call. I am sorry that I've been interrupted because I had hoped to clear this matter up with you on this telephone conversation, but, as I say, the police insist on having the right-of-way."

Mason hung up the telephone and turned to Lt. Tragg. "What can I do for you this morning, Lieutenant?"

Tragg turned to the plain-clothes man and said, "I guess you know Perry Mason. That's Paul Drake, his detective, and Della Street, the very estimable secretary who chaperones his affairs. Don't underestimate the intelligence of any one of them, particularly don't be misled by that look of innocence on the part of Miss Street or those very, very beautiful eyes which somehow seem to get your thoughts off things you're trying to accomplish.

"Would you mind telling me with whom you were talking, Perry?"

"A client," Mason said.

"Good heavens!" Tragg exclaimed in mock surprise. "I thought from what I heard of the conversation it was a total stranger, someone who rang you up and wanted to know how to get to the post office from here or if you happened to know what the bus fare was to San Diego."

"It just goes to show a person can be misled jumping at conclusions. A good detective should never jump at conclusions," Mason said.

Tragg said, "Mason, I understand you have a client by the name of Gilman, Carter Gilman."

Mason said, "If you say you have a certain understanding, I see no reason to doubt the statement."

"Well, then, let me ask you—*do* you have a client by the name of Carter Gilman?"

Mason frowned as though trying to prod his memory. "Gilman . . . Gilman," he said, "Carter Gilman. Do you happen to know his address?"

"6231 Vauxman Avenue," Tragg said.

"Well," Mason said, "we could look it up and . . . no, Tragg, I don't think I should answer that question."

Tragg turned to the man in plain clothes and said, "Notice the cleverness of the guy. He acts as though he hadn't heard of Carter Gilman in a month of Sundays and then, having put on that act, he tells me that he isn't going to answer the question. In that way, he hasn't lied to me, he hasn't said anything that wasn't so, he simply played it cute."

Tragg turned back to Mason. "Mason," he said, "I am asking you now an official question. Have you removed any incriminating evidence from the premises at 6231 Vauxman Avenue—from any part of the premises?"

"Incriminating evidence," Mason said. "Now, let's see what we mean by that. Evidence, of course, is something that is legally admissible in the way of proof, and that, of course, calls for legal definition.

"Now, incriminating is something else again. I would have to ask incriminating to whom.

"You see, Tragg, since you want to play games this morning, there are lots of things that you might consider evidence which a court wouldn't technically consider evidence because it wouldn't be admissible."

"I know," Tragg said. "Hearsay, for instance."

"Well, there again," Mason said, "you are up against certain exceptions. For instance, if a man asked you how old you were and you'd say fifty-five, perhaps—now, of course, you have no way of knowing that you're fifty-five except because of something someone has told you. So you'd be testifying to something that was purely hearsay. Yet that is one of the exceptions to the hearsay evidence rule which the layman never stops to think about."

"Well, now," Tragg said, "I see we're going to have rather a prolonged visit. I—"

The telephone rang again. Della Street picked up the receiver, said, "Yes," then gave Mason a meaning glance. "Perhaps you'd better take this call in the law library," she said.

"Oh, now, you don't have to do anything like that," Tragg said. "We're not trying to eavesdrop, but we *are* in something of a hurry and the business might be described as official, so perhaps you'd just better answer the phone, Perry, and tell whoever is calling to call back."

Mason caught the expression on Della Street's face, picked up the telephone, said, "Hello," and heard the voice of Carter Gilman.

"Mr. Mason, this is Carter Gilman. I am being held on suspicion of murder. They've interrogated me at the district attorney's office and I am now being booked. They told me that I had a right to call my attorney, so I'm calling you."

Mason said, "I'll be right down to see you. Now, in the

meantime, I don't know what you've said to anybody, but from now on you aren't to say a thing unless I'm there. Do you understand? You're not to open your mouth unless I give you permission—not even to talk about the weather. Don't give anyone the time of day. I'll be there just as soon as I can get there."

Mason hung up the telephone.

Tragg turned sadly to the man standing beside him and said, "That's what comes of all these recent decisions about depriving a man of due process of law; when you restrain him without taking him before a magistrate, when you don't give him an opportunity to call his attorney before you've even talked with him.

"The whole law-enforcement business has gone completely cockeyed. They're taking the handcuffs off the wrists of the criminals and putting them on the wrists of the law-enforcement officers.

"Well, I guess the cat's out of the bag, Mason. I presume that you're not going to answer any more questions, that you're going to clap on your hat, shoot out of that door and dash down to the jail to confer with your client. Well, we can't stop you, Mason. *So far,* we don't have anything on you, but we're looking around, Perry, we're looking around."

Mason said, "Keep on looking, Lieutenant. By the way, I presume you have your official car out here and you're probably on your way to the jail. Now, if you wanted to be really hospitable and a good sport about this thing you'd give me a ride with you and I'd save quite a bit of time."

"To say nothing of taxi fare," Tragg said. "It's quite all

right, Perry. Just to show you that we're good sports, we'll take you right through traffic and right up to where you can visit your client.

"Of course, you understand, Perry, I can't use the code signal that calls for red light and siren. I'll have to go just as an ordinary law-abiding citizen, but we know our way around and we can expedite things for you. It will look nice in case you should claim your client was deprived of due process of law or that the police restrained him unduly trying to get a confession out of him.

"Come right along with us, Perry, and we'll see that you're delivered F.O.B. the county jail, where you can talk with your client, who is being held on suspicion of murdering Vera Martel. And I don't mind telling you privately and confidentially, Perry, that this time we have an ironclad case, and unless you're very, very careful you're going to find yourself involved along with your client—right up to your necktie."

Mason bowed. "Thank you for the warning and the ride, Lieutenant."

Mason turned to Della Street and said, half jokingly, half seriously, "If you don't hear from me within an hour make an application for a writ of habeas corpus."

Della Street nodded solemnly.

Paul Drake, who had been a silent spectator, held the door open for the three men to go out.

CHAPTER EIGHT

PERRY MASON sat in the counsel room at the county jail and looked across at Carter Gilman as the latter entered the room.

"All right, Gilman," Mason said. "What seems to be the trouble?"

"Mr. Mason, I don't know. I swear I don't."

"Save the swearing until you get in front of a jury," Mason said. "Then you'll have to be sworn. Now, tell me what happened."

"I had been in Las Vegas and came in on an early plane. I was supposed to be at the office this morning, but I thought I'd go to the house first. However, I never got there. Police were waiting at the airport and they picked me up and said they wanted to question me."

"What about?"

"About the death of Vera Martel."

"You know she's dead, then?"

"Oh, yes. They told me that."

"And what did you tell them?"

"I told them that . . . well, I finally admitted that I had been to see you about Vera Martel."

"Oh, you did, did you? And why did you tell them you had been to see me?"

"Because I thought she was trying to blackmail some member of the family."

"Now you say some member of the family," Mason said. "Originally you told me she was trying to blackmail your wife."

"Well, I've been thinking things over."

"All right," Mason said, "go on. What else?"

"Well, they asked me about my workshop and what kind of woods I'd been working with and where I bought my woods, and they asked me what I'd been doing in Las Vegas."

"What were you doing?"

"Gambling."

"Win anything?"

"No."

"How much did you lose?"

"I guess I just about broke even."

"Rather an uneventful trip," Mason said.

"Well, I had my ups and downs."

"Did they ask you when you first learned Vera Martel was trying to blackmail some member of the family?"

"Oh, yes. They asked me everything."

"And what did you tell them in answer to that question?"

"I told them that I had seen Miss Martel's car parked near my office on two occasions and near my house once. I also said a Miss Martel had called the house a couple of times."

"Those were times when you were home alone?"

"Yes."

"And you asked Vera Martel for her name?"

"She gave her name and said for Mrs. Gilman to call as soon as she came in."

"And you gave your wife those messages?" Mason asked.

Gilman hesitated.

"Now look," Mason said, "let's quit beating around the bush. I don't think Vera Martel was ever inside your house, I don't think she ever called your wife. I'm pretty certain that you never delivered any messages to your wife saying that she had called and that your wife will so tell the police.

"Now, what happened is that Roger Calhoun hired Vera Martel because he had heard there was some sort of a scandal connected with Glamis and he wanted to find out what it was.

"Vera Martel dug up something and then she decided to play it smart. She started playing both ends against the middle. She wanted to know how much Roger Calhoun was willing to pay to get the information and how much you were willing to pay not to have her give it to Calhoun.

"So," Mason went on, "yesterday morning you had a date with Vera Martel. She was to meet you in your workroom. You were to pay her ten thousand dollars. She came a little earlier than you expected and you wanted to get away from Muriell's field of vision, so, despite the fact you'd eaten a full breakfast, you sent Muriell back to the kitchen to do some more cooking—"

"Good heavens! How do you know all this?" Gilman interrupted.

"I make it my business to know things," Mason said. "You got up and left the table. You went out to the workshop. Vera Martel took the ten thousand dollars and then told you she wanted some additional money. You lost your temper and flew at her in a rage. She may have pulled a knife or a gun. You choked her and then, frightened to death at what had happened, stuffed her body in the trunk of your car, drove out to where you could hide the body. Then you went back and got Vera Martel's car where it had been parked near your place, and . . ."

Gilman was shaking his head emphatically.

"Just listen for a while," Mason said. "You got her car, drove out on Mulholland Drive, put her body in the car, ran the car over the grade.

"Then you decided you'd start building an alibi for yourself. You had an appointment with me at eleven thirty. You did your best to try and make it, but you had been doing a lot. You were a few minutes late.

"So you told me this story about Vera Martel and about what you wanted me to do, knowing all the time that Vera Martel was dead. Then you went out and started building your alibi. You arranged to have someone with you all the time. You didn't know just when Vera Martel's body would be discovered, but you knew that the longer you could postpone discovery the better chance you had.

"So you decided to trap me and use me as a witness to show that Vera Martel had been alive some time after she was actually murdered. So you fixed up a message with your secretary about your fingerprints, and had your secretary, whom you felt you could trust, call me from a telephone pay station at Graystone 9-3535—that's only a few blocks from your office. You had your secretary call me from that station while you were standing beside her. You had her try to disguise her voice by talking rapidly and say that she was Vera Martel, that you had been to see me, that you had given me the name of Edward Carter, that actually you were Carter Gilman, that you were a fool, that I was to ring you at that number and give you a message about fingerprints.

"So I rang you up at that number. I gave you that message and you pretended to be tremendously impressed by it and very frightened. You hesitated and you wanted to know how in the world Vera Martel could have known you were there unless you were being shadowed. Then, after you had put on a pretty good act, you hung up and your secretary called the office to see if you had come in yet. You dashed back to whatever place it was where you were building an alibi, probably a conference with some banker since that pay station is within three blocks of a branch bank where you do business.

"Later on, you went to Las Vegas. The records of the airplane company will show what plane you took. Once in Las Vegas you didn't need to be quite so careful. Now, I don't know what you went there for, but I wouldn't be too surprised if it wasn't to try and get into the office of Vera Martel to look for incriminating documents.

"That's generally the plan you had worked out. By following it, you've bought yourself a one-way ticket to the gas chamber. Your secretary is loyal and she'd do just about anything you asked her, but when she finds out that she's given a choice of being an accessory after the fact in a murder or telling the police the truth, she'll tell the truth. They're probably grilling her right now.

"If you'd called me as soon as it happened and had given me the facts, I might have been able to do something to help you. We might at least have made it look like manslaughter or second-degree murder. But now, with all this elaborate skulduggery you've worked out, you've made the whole thing appear to be premeditated murder and they're going to get a verdict of first-degree murder."

Mason quit talking and let his eyes bore into Gilman's panic-stricken eyes.

"Well?" Mason asked at length.

Gilman shook his head.

"All right," Mason said, "What's the truth?"

"I'll tell it to you," Gilman said, "but I won't tell it to any other living soul. I won't go on the witness stand. I won't even admit it if you should ask me."

"All right," Mason said. "Go on, tell me what happened."

"I'm—I'm protecting someone; someone I love very much."

"Who?" Mason asked.

Gilman shook his head.

"Who?" Mason asked.

"All right," Gilman blurted, "I'm protecting a member of my family."

"That's a little better," Mason said. "Now perhaps we can do something. Tell me what happened."

"I was eating breakfast," Gilman said. "I knew that Vera Martel was trying to find out something about the family."

"How did you know that?"

"I'll come to that in a minute."

"All right," Mason said. "What happened at breakfast?"

"I saw Vera Martel hurry down the driveway and enter Nancy's darkroom."

"Go on," Mason said.

"I was absolutely thunderstruck," Gilman said, "to think that she would come to my house. I knew then that the situation was very desperate, that there was something in the nature of a pay-off that was taking place.

"I intended to go down the driveway and have a showdown with Vera Martel.

"Now, this is important, Mr. Mason, and you must remember it. In order to keep from arousing Muriell's suspicions I didn't dare to sit there just looking out the window. I had to be pretending to read my paper, so I can't swear to exactly what happened. I was looking at the paper part of the time."

"Go on."

"I got Muriell out in the kitchen cooking and I got up quietly from the table, dropped the paper on the floor and was about to tiptoe out of the front door when I looked out of the window and saw . . ."

"Yes," Mason said.

"I saw a member of my family running from the workshop with a face that was indicative of panic."

"Who was it?" Mason asked.

Gilman shook his head. "I'll never tell even you that, Mason, because I know that if you take my case you're going to try to save my bacon, and as an ethical lawyer you'll save it at the expense of anyone whom you think is guilty."

"All right," Mason said, "we'll let it go at that for a while. You saw a member of your family coming out of the workshop. So then what happened?"

"Then I hurried out of the front door. I ran on tiptoe along the cement driveway. I opened the door to the darkroom and hurried across the darkroom to the door to the workshop. I opened that and at what I saw nearly fainted."

"What did you see?"

"There was a pool of crimson on the floor which at first I took to be blood. There was a broken chair. There was money all over the floor of the workshop—hundred-dollar bills just scattered everywhere."

"All right, go on," Mason said. "What did you do?"

"I dropped my napkin, I guess. I just stood there. Then I saw that the pool of red I had thought was blood was actually red enamel which was leaking from the loose cap of a can of red enamel which had been knocked off the workbench. I went over and picked up the can and put it back on the shelf right side up. Then I realized what must have happened."

"What must have happened?" Mason asked.

"This member of my family had gone out with a lot of money in hundred-dollar bills to pay for blackmail and . . . well, Vera Martel had raised the ante and there had been violence."

"So what did you do? Did you ask this member of the family about it?"

"I did not," Gilman said. "I ran and jumped in my car and started the motor and started looking for Vera Martel. I knew she couldn't have gone far. I circled the block, then I cruised around the various streets and I couldn't find her, but I did find her car parked within a half a block of the house."

"How did you know it was her car?"

"It had a Nevada license on it."

"How did you know it was her car?" Mason asked.

"It . . . all right, I'll tell you the rest of it. Roger Calhoun *did* hire Vera Martel to find out something about a scandal in the family. My secretary, Matilda Norman ,who has been with me for some time and is intensely loyal, found out about it from Roger's secretary when a few words came in over the intercom before Calhoun realized it was open. For your information, Roger Calhoun's secretary, Miss Colfax, hates his guts, but she has to play up to him because she's drawing about twice the ordinary salary. However, she found out enough to know that Roger had Vera Martel in there and was going to pay her money to find out something about the family and she knew that Vera Martel came from Nevada."

"So what?"

"So she came and told Matilda Norman, and Tillie told me."

"And you," Mason asked, "busted in on Calhoun and Vera Martel and asked him what the hell he thought he was doing?"

"That's what I should have done," Gilman said. "I'm afraid I did the wrong thing."

"What did you do?"

"I wanted to find out more about what was going on, so I went down to the parking lot and looked around for cars with a Nevada license. I found one and I really gave it the works. I found keys in a key container in the lock and looked in the key container and found an identifying tag of Vera Martel with a Las Vegas address."

"Go on," Mason said.

"There was some modeling clay in my car. I went over

to it, took out the clay and made an impression of the keys in the key container."

"What did you do that for?" Mason asked.

"I simply don't know," Gilman said. "I just wanted to find out everything I could. I was in a panic at the idea that some scandal might be uncovered in connection with my family.

"I've known for a long time that there might have been something a little irregular—that is, a little premature about the birth of Glamis, but . . . that wouldn't have been enough. It had to be something in addition to that, and I wanted to find out what it was."

"So you got the idea that while Vera Martel was available you'd make duplicate keys and go over and search her office?"

Gilman hesitated a moment, then nodded.

"You certainly have stuck your neck in a noose," Mason said. "Is that what you were doing last night?"

"Yes."

"What did you find?"

"I found that somebody had beat me to it," Gilman blurted. "The office was a wreck. Papers were scattered all over the floor. You couldn't find anything in the filing case in any kind of order. All of the papers had been mixed up. Someone had pulled everything out and just thrown them helter-skelter on the floor."

"Did you have sense enough to wear gloves?" Mason asked.

The look of dismay on Gilman's face was Mason's answer.

"All right," Mason said. "You probably left fingerprints all over the place. You've given them the most perfect first-degree murder case Hamilton Burger ever had. There's only one peculiar thing about all this and that is that I am halfway inclined to believe you. . . . Now, what did you do when you finished cruising around yesterday morning looking for Vera Martel? You say you found her car parked within half a block of your place. What did you do with your car?"

"I drove to the place where I usually take the bus and parked my car on the side street."

"That's how far from your house?"

"About four blocks."

"All right. You left the car there. Then what did you do?"

"I didn't know what to do, Mr. Mason. I was in a daze. I took a bus for the office, but I never went there. I walked around for some time, then I decided to go home and have a showdown with my family. So I got on the bus and went back almost to my house, and then suddenly realized that I had that appointment with you and that I had better go and see you, that I could dump the whole thing in your lap. So I got off the bus, caught another bus back and came up to your office to keep my appointment.

"Now, you're wrong about me having Matilda Norman ring you up to make you think that Vera Martel was alive at that time. I was afraid that you might be working a little too leisurely. I wanted to give you a challenge. I knew that if Vera Martel made it seem she was outwitting you, you'd get on the job and do something about it. So I fixed up this scheme with my secretary . . . but how in the world you found out who it was calling is more than I'll ever know."

Mason said, "There's no time for you to ask me questions. I'm asking you questions. You try to answer them. There were three people beside yourself in that house—Muriell, your wife and Glamis. Since Muriell was up and cooking the breakfast she could well be the one you saw running out of the workshop. That's rather an interesting possibility."

"Actually, there were four people beside myself in the house," Gilman said.

"Who was the fourth?"

"A young man from up in the northern part of the state somewhere. Hartley Elliott, a rather personable young chap, a manufacturers' agent."

"What about him?"

"He has been going with Glamis and he escorted her home at some time around two or thee o'clock in the morning. . . . The way young people do things these days really gets me."

"Go on," Mason said.

"Well, as I get the story now, he parked his car and went up and sat on the porch with Glamis for a while and he left the ignition on in the car. When he came back to turn the ignition key into the starting position, the battery simply refused to take hold, so Glamis suggested that he come on up and spend the night in one of the guest rooms."

"How many guest rooms?"

"Two."

"Where are they?"

"Upstairs, on the north side. The guest room that he occupied was directly over the dining room. As a matter of fact, I heard him moving around up there and that tended to confuse me. I didn't know that he had spent the night there . . . not until later."

"How much later?"

"Last night, when I called Muriell from Las Vegas. Muriell was very much concerned about me and I could see that she was curious about me. . . . Well, we talked for some little time on the telephone and she told me about Hartley Elliott staying there overnight."

"You paid for the call?" Mason asked.

"No, I didn't. I called collect."

"From Las Vegas?"

"Yes. I asked for Muriell and told the operator to reverse the charges."

"So, in case they were needing any more clues," Mason said, "they have a long-distance call to help out."

Gilman said, "Mr. Mason, if I have to, I'll plead guilty. You can make some sort of a deal with the prosecutor by which I can plead guilty to manslaughter, and then, what with my position and background, I can get out in a year or two."

Mason said, "You listen to me. I'll tell you what you can do and what you can't do when the time comes. In the meantime, you don't say one single word to anybody about pleading guilty to anything. You just keep your mouth completely, entirely shut. You tell everybody that your attorney has given you instructions not to discuss the case in any way, not to discuss your family, not to discuss your background, not to discuss your business. Now then, I want to know one thing. Did you kill her?"

"Mr. Mason, honestly I did not."

"But you felt she probably had been killed, and you are morally certain that someone in your family did kill her?"

"Yes."

"Was it Muriell?"

"I am not going to answer."

"Was it Glamis?"

"I won't be cross-examined."

"Was it your wife?"

"I've told you, Mr. Mason, that I am not going to ever tell anybody. That name will never pass my lips as long as I'm alive."

"Was it Hartley Elliott?"

"Heavens, no. I wouldn't take a rap simply to protect him."

"Well," Mason said, "you're either a devoted husband, father and stepfather, or else you're a damn good actor. And right at the moment I don't know which, but I intend to find out.

"Now, you sit tight, and under no circumstances discuss the case with anyone."

"Where are you going now?"

"I'm going out to your house," Mason said. "I'm going to talk with the various members of the family, and while I'm talking with them I'm going to try to make up my mind whether any one of them is lying, and, if so, which one it is. And if none of them are lying I'll feel pretty certain that you murdered Vera Martel out in your workshop and have concocted a story that is designed to arouse my sympathy and cause me to use my best efforts in softening up the district attorney so you can, as they say in crook parlance, cop a plea."

And Mason turned, signaling to the guard that the interview was over.

CHAPTER NINE

MASON PARKED his car in front of the residence on Vauxman Avenue, hurried up the front steps and was about to press the doorbell when the door was flung open by Muriell Gilman.

"Oh, Mr. Mason, what is it?" she asked. "Tell me."

"I'll tell all of you at once," Mason said. "How about the others—are they up?"

She shook her head. "I did what you said, Mr. Mason. I let them sleep on."

"That's fine," Mason said. "Now get them up and tell them to come down here. I have some important news. I want to have them all together when I tell you."

"But, Mr. Mason, tell me, is Daddy . . . Daddy hasn't been hurt . . . or—or killed?"

"Physically," Mason said, "your father is quite safe at the moment. I have some news and I'm not going to have it dragged out of me piecemeal. I want you all together when I tell you the news and I want to have Nancy and Glamis down here so I can talk with them at the same time I talk with you."

"Glamis is a savage before she has her coffee," Muriell said. "I'd better take her some coffee."

"You get her down here and let her be savage," Mason said. "Tell her I want to talk with her."

Muriell said, "Come on in, Mr. Mason, and I'll get Nancy and Glamis down here."

Mason followed her into a big, tastefully arranged living room.

"Can I take a look at the dining room and kitchen while you're upstairs?" Mason asked.

"Why, certainly. Let me run up and tell Nancy and Glamis. I'm satisfied you'll have a little time before they get some clothes on, get presentable and get down here. If you'll just wait, please."

"I'll wait," Mason said, "but I'm going to look around."

Muriell hurried up the staircase. Mason glanced briefly around the living room, then walked to the dining room, pushed back the swinging door to the kitchen, looked in the kitchen, studying the location of the doors and windows, and was back in the dining room by the time Muriell returned.

"Did you get them up?" he asked.

"I got them awake," she said. "Nancy is coming right down. I don't know about Glamis. She was *really* put out."

"That's too bad," Mason said casually. "Now, I notice that standing here in the dining room you can look out at the garage and the workshop, but you can't see them from the kitchen."

"That's right. The dining-room wall makes a little jog right here and you can see the garage and workshop through that window."

"Where was your father sitting?"

"Right near where you're standing, right there at that place at the table."

"Then he could have seen the workshop from the window while he was eating breakfast."

"Yes, I guess so."

"But *you* couldn't see out from the kitchen?"

"No, the kitchen door opens onto a service porch— You can see the workshop and garage from the door of the service porch, however, but you can't see out from the kitchen. Why, Mr. Mason? Does it make any difference?"

"I don't know." Mason said. "I'm trying to get the picture—and it's rather a confused picture right at the moment. I'm hoping your stepmother can—"

"Can do what?" a woman's voice asked.

Mason turned to encounter the curious, slightly indignant eyes of a tall, blond woman who, despite the lack of make-up and the fact that she apparently was dressed only in a housecoat and slippers, was remarkably attractive.

"I'm hoping," Mason said, "you can clear up certain matters for me."

"I hope so, too. I'm Nancy Gilman. I understand you are Perry Mason, the noted lawyer, and that you have some very important news for me about my husband. I didn't stop for make-up or anything, I just put on a housecoat and slippers, and here I am, Mr. Mason. I'm certainly hoping that the information you have is sufficiently important to justify an invasion of this sort at this hour of the morning."

Mason reached a sudden decision. He said, "All right, I'll hand it to you straight from the shoulder. Your husband, Carter Gilman, is in jail."

"For heaven's sakes! What's he been doing?"

Mason said, "The authorities think he's guilty of murder."

"Of murder!"

"That's right."

Nancy Gilman drew out a chair and seated herself. She looked at Mason long and earnestly, then shook her head and said, "There's something completely fantastic about all this, Mr. Mason. You don't seem to be the drinking type. Are you sure of your facts?"

"I have just come from visiting him in the jail," Mason said.

"May I ask what this murder is all about—drunken car-driving, or what?"

Mason, watching her closely, said, "Apparently he is accused of the deliberate, willful murder of Vera M. Martel."

Nancy Gilman's eyebrows went up. She looked inquiringly at Muriell, then back at Mason. "And who is Vera M. Martel?"

"A private detective who may have been blackmailing you," Mason said, standing with his shoulders squared, his weight on the balls of his feet, his manner indicating impatient disapproval of Nancy Gilman's attitude and his intention of forcing the truth out of her.

"Blackmailing me?"

"That's the general idea."

Nancy Gilman shook her head. "Nobody's been blackmailing me, Mr. Mason."

"Or trying to?"

Again there was a shake of the head.

"What about the ten thousand dollars?" Mason asked.

"What ten thousand dollars? Mr. Mason, you have a peculiar attitude. It's the attitude of someone who is trying to force an unwilling witness to give out information."

"What attitude would you suggest?" Mason asked.

"Really, I don't know, Mr. Mason. I know who you are, of course, and your reputation; otherwise, I wouldn't have come down here. I hardly feel qualified to tell you how to practice law but your manner arouses my curiosity and, if you'll pardon my frankness, a certain instinctive resentment."

"All right," Mason said, "have all the resentment you want. Let's get the facts straight. There's no time to play cat and mouse with a situation of this sort. The police are going to be out here at any minute and they're going to question you. You have an attractive personality, are evidently quite accustomed to dominate any situation in which you find yourself by using personality and sex appeal, both of which commodities are of no value in dealing with the police. For your information, the police don't play games."

"I'm not playing games, Mr. Mason."

"Do you know anything about ten thousand dollars in cash?"

"What am I supposed to know about it?"

"Did you know your husband drew that money from his bank?"

She shook her head.

"Did you draw it from your bank?"

"Heavens, no!"

"Did you have ten thousand dollars in cash within the last few days?"

"Certainly not."

"Have you ever had any conversation with Vera M. Martel?"

"I wouldn't know her from any woman I'd meet on the street. You say she's a private detective?"

"A private detective," Mason said, "and she may have been a blackmailer. The police have reason to believe she was choked to death in the workshop out in back of the house and that ten thousand dollars, which was intended to be used as a bribe or a blackmail payment, was left in the workshop while someone went out to dispose of Vera Martel's body."

"Mr. Mason, you seem sober, you seem serious and what you're saying at least seems logical to you, but from my standpoint I'd say you were either drunk, had been taking dope, or were completely crazy."

Glamis Barlow swept into the room imperiously. She was attired in a filmy negligee which silhouetted her long legs and the curves of her body, and she was angry.

"May I ask what in the world this is all about?" she asked.

Mason said, "I wanted to question you."

"Well, question me at some decent hour then," she said, "and don't think I have to answer your questions just because I was attracted by you yesterday. Today you're a pain in the anatomy. Now what's this all about?"

Nancy said, "Carter has been arrested for murder, Glamis."

"For murder!"

Nancy nodded. "So Mr. Mason insists. It seems a woman named . . . what was that name again, Mr. Mason?"

"Vera M. Martel," Mason said.

"Mr. Mason seems to think a woman named Martel was murdered out in the workshop," Nancy Gilman said.

Glamis looked at the lawyer with eyes that were like blue ice. "Mr. Mason, is this your idea of a joke or are you trying to get some information out of us and have chosen a shock approach in order to do it?"

Muriell, hurrying in from the kitchen with a cup of steaming coffee, said, "Here, honey, have some coffee."

Glamis made no effort to reach for the coffee cup, no effort to thank Muriell. She simply ignored Muriell as though the girl had no existence, and continued to hold Perry Mason with a fixed stare of hostility.

"I'm waiting for an answer, Mr. Mason," she said.

Mason said, "Listen, I've told your mother and I'm telling you—we aren't playing games here. We don't have much time. The police are going to be here within a few minutes and, believe me, when you start talking with the police you'll come face to face with reality.

"Now, you can start in answering some direct questions and avoiding all histrionics. Do you know Vera M. Martel?"

"No!" she spat at him.

"Did you ever pay Vera Martel any money?"

"No."

"Do you know anything about ten thousand dollars in cash which was supposed to have been found in the workshop?"

"No."

"Did you go to your bank and get ten thousand dollars in cash any time within the past few days?"

"No."

"Have you ever had any conversations with a Vera Martel?"

"No."

"Do you know who she is?"

"No."

"All right," Mason said, "let's get this thing straight. Do any one of the three of you know anything about Vera Martel?"

"I certainly don't," Glamis snapped.

"And you?" Mason asked Nancy.

"Don't be silly, Mr. Mason. I've told you half a dozen times, I don't know her. I don't know anything about her. I never had anything to do with her, and I don't propose to be sitting here in my own house and be browbeaten by some attorney."

Mason said, "You make just one wrong answer to the police and you're all going to be in this thing up to your necks. What's more, you're going to drag Carter Gilman into the gas chamber. Remember that the police have ways of tracing these things. Murder isn't a parlor game that you play according to rules.

"Now you, Glamis, got in your car after you left me, drove to the airport and went to Las Vegas."

"So you *were* having me shadowed! I wondered about it. As it happens, I go to Las Vegas every so often."

"And what did you do in Las Vegas?"

"I gambled, I saw my father, Steven Barlow, and I came home. I had some drinks, I lost some money and I minded my own business—a most commendable habit, Mr. Mason. I would suggest that *you* try it sometime."

The door chimes sounded.

Muriell started for the front door.

"Just a minute," Mason said. He held Glamis Barlow with his eyes. "Vera Martel had an office in Las Vegas. Did you call on her or try to call on her at that office? Did you go near the place?"

"Mr. Mason, don't be silly. I tell you, I don't know any Vera Martel, so why should I go to her office?"

The door chimes sounded again and then there was a knock on the door.

"That," Mason said, "sounds very much like my friend, Lieutenant Arthur Tragg of Homicide. May I suggest that when you talk with him you either keep very, very quiet or you answer questions truthfully. Don't try lying. That's going to get you in all sorts of trouble.

"Now, then, I want all three of you to tell me you are, and each of you is, giving me all of your right, title and interest to any and all money that was in the workshop yesterday."

"Why should we give it to you?" Glamis asked.

"Not the money," Mason said, "only your title to the money. If it wasn't yours you wouldn't be giving me anything."

Again the door chimes sounded and peremptory knuckles banged on the door, alternating with the door chimes.

"All right," Nancy said. "We're all agreed, girls?"

The two girls nodded.

"Have any of you pawned any diamonds, jewelry or raised any cash by any emergency loans?" Mason asked. "Remember, that's one thing the police can trace just as surely as—"

Angry knuckles pounded on the front door and simultaneously there was the sound of knuckles on the back door, then the back door opened and a police officer pushed his way through the kitchen into the dining room. "Why don't you folks answer the doorbell?" he asked.

He strode across the dining room to the living room, opened the door and said, "Come on in, Lieutenant."

Mason lowered his voice. "Don't tell anyone anything about any money. Don't tell anyone I was asking about any money."

Mason looked from one to the other, let his eyes rest for a long moment on Muriell.

Lt. Tragg entered the room, said, "Pardon me, ladies, but I'm after some information and . . . I see that Mr. Perry Mason has been briefing you on what happened. . . . I noted your car was parked in the driveway, Perry.

"After all, this is a free country and we don't try to keep an attorney from conferring with his clients or even briefing friendly witnesses. But we don't like to be left cooling our heels out on the front porch while the session is unduly protracted.

"Now, Mr. Mason, since you've had ample opportunity to talk to these witnesses, I think that it's only fair that I be given an opportunity to discuss things with them privately. We're going to excuse you."

"And if I don't choose to go?" Mason asked. "Are you going to put me out?"

"Good heavens, no, nothing like that," Tragg said. "I'm simply going to put a police guard at the door of one of these rooms and question these women in the room with a police guard seeing that we're not disturbed— Or I can, of course, take the witnesses to Headquarters for examination, which will cause a certain amount of newspaper publicity which your client might find objectionable."

Glamis reached over to pick up the coffee cup which Muriell had deposited on the dining-room table. She smiled provocatively at Lt. Tragg and said, "I like men who use direct action, Lieutenant."

"Good," Lt. Tragg said, appraising her unsmilingly. "Then I'll talk with you first, before you've had your coffee."

Tragg took the coffee.

Glamis became white-faced. "You beast!" she spat.

The officer took Mason's arm. "I'll escort you to the door, Mr. Mason. I'm quite certain Lieutenant Tragg doesn't feel your presence would by of any help."

Mason jerked himself free, swung around and said, "Just a minute. You may have the right to examine these witnesses in private and you may not. I'm not certain that I'm going to let you get away with it, and I'm not certain that I won't tell all of these witnesses not to answer any questions."

"On what grounds?" Tragg asked. "On the grounds that to do so might incriminate them?"

"They don't have to give any grounds," Mason said. "They don't have to answer questions, period."

"That's right, they don't," Tragg said. "Of course, when they're subpoenaed in front of a grand jury they either have to answer questions or take refuge in the fact that the answers might incriminate them."

Mason turned to the women. "I've talked with you," he said. "I've told you the circumstances. I'm going to warn you—don't tell any lies to Lieutenant Tragg. Either tell him the truth or tell him nothing."

"A very, very commendable attitude," Lt. Tragg said. And then added somewhat wistfully, "I do wish I knew what had taken place before we got here. You see, Perry, we were running down another angle of the case which we considered of prime importance; even of more importance then questioning the members of Mr. Gilman's family.

"I'm sorry that I can't tell you what that angle is, but you'll doubtless discover it by the time you get to court. I can assure you of one thing, Perry. It's a dilly."

"It must have been," Mason said, "to cause you to postpone a trip out here."

Mason walked to the door, turned, said, "Remember what I told you. Either tell him the truth or keep silent, and don't volunteer any information. Answer his questions and then quit."

CHAPTER TEN

MASON STOPPED at the first telephone booth, called his office, and when he had Della Street on the line, asked, "What do you hear from Paul Drake? Has he dug up anything?"

"He's located Glamis' boy friend, Hartley Elliott," Della Street said, "and has been calling frantically. He says he's sitting on the lid and that you'll have to get out there just as fast as you can."

"What's the address?" Mason asked.

"The Rossiter Apartments on Blendon Street."

"What's the number, Della?"

"7211. The apartment is 6-B, and Paul seems terribly concerned."

"If he calls in again," Mason said, "tell him I'm on my way. Also, tell him that Tragg and a uniformed officer have just descended on the Gilman family at their home on Vauxman Avenue, and it looks as though the party is going to get rough."

"I'll tell him. Did you have a chance to get anything worth while before Tragg moved in on you?" Della Street asked.

"There's something peculiar about the case," Mason said. "I can't put my finger on it yet— I had a chance to ask questions and get some negative answers. I'm not certain the negatives mean anything. I'll be on my way to join Paul. I'll call you as soon as I have anything new."

Mason hung up the telephone, jumped in his car and drove to the Rossiter Apartments, went at once to Apartment 6-B and knocked on the door.

Paul Drake opened the door.

There was no mistaking the expression of relief on Paul Drake's face when he saw Mason in the doorway.

Drake said, "Come in and take over, Perry."

A tall, slim-waisted man, about twenty-eight years old, with high cheekbones, steady gray eyes, a determined jaw and the build of an athlete was standing by the window.

"This is Mr. Mason, Elliott," Paul Drake said.

Elliott eyed the attorney appraisingly, bowed, and after a moment moved slowly forward so that when he shook hands with Mason the lawyer had covered two thirds of the distance.

"Mr. Elliott," Paul Drake went on, lowering his left eyelid in a wink that only Mason could see, "is friendly with Glamis Barlow. In fact, they've been keeping company and Elliott spent the night out there Tuesday night. That was it, wasn't it, Elliott—Tuesday?"

"You know it was," Elliott said coldly. "It was yesterday morning. Are you trying to trap me in some way? I didn't spend the night there. I spent the morning there."

"Just trying to keep the date straight," Drake said cheerfully.

Mason stood by Hartley Elliott, who didn't ask either Mason or Drake to sit down.

Elliott folded his arms across his chest. "The date was the thirteenth," he said stiffly.

Drake said, "By way of explanation, Perry, Hartley

Elliott and Glamis got home early and it was rather a warm night. They went up on the porch for a while, then he came in and had a drink with Glamis. When he went out to start his car he found that he had inadvertently left the ignition on. The car wouldn't start. To make a long story short, he stayed all night."

"I see," Mason said.

"Now, before we go any further," Elliott said coldly, "let me state that I prefer to do my own talking. I don't know just what the situation is, but I don't care to have any private detective putting words in my mouth and I don't know that I care to talk with any lawyer until after I've seen my own attorney. I'm willing to listen, but that's all."

"You seem rather truculent," Mason said. "Is something wrong?"

"How do I know?" Elliott said. "I'm minding my own business and in comes a private detective asking a lot of questions about Glamis, about where I've been and what I've been doing, and then he telephones the office of an attorney and leaves word for the attorney to join him. I've indicated to Mr. Drake a couple of times that he doesn't need to stay here on my account but he's been persistent in questioning me and persistent in waiting for you. I finally agreed that I would wait for you because Drake said you would explain everything.

"Now, as far as I'm concerned, you can start explaining."

Mason said, "I'd like to know a little more about just what happened yesterday morning and—"

"I think you heard me," Elliott said. "I want you to start explaining."

Mason glanced at Paul Drake, then said abruptly, "All right, I'll start explaining because we may not have much time. If you stayed in that house yesterday morning, you may not have very much time left for informal conversation.

"Do you know a person named Vera M. Martel?"

"I told you to start explaining," Elliott said. "I don't care to answer any more questions until there's been a little explaining."

"All right," Mason said. "Vera M. Martel was found dead in her automobile on a canyon road in the mountains. At first, the police thought it was a highway acciden, then they didn't like the looks of things and thought perhaps the car had been deliberately run over a cliff with a body in it. So they performed an autopsy and, so far, they've found petechial hemorrhages of the eyeball and a broken hyoid bone, which are all strongly indicative of manual strangulation.

"They also found some peculiar bits of sawdust in her shoes. Microscopic examination showed the sawdust didn't come from ordinary lumber but from a very rare type of lumber, and the police think they have traced that rare type of lumber to the workshop of Carter Gilman.

"At the moment, Carter Gilman is in jail, being held for suspicion of first-degree murder, the police are at the Gilman residence at Vauxman Avenue and we're trying to get something out of you that may help before the police get here."

Elliott glanced from Mason to Drake, then moved over to a chair and sat down suddenly as though his knees had buckled.

"Want any more?" Mason asked.

Elliott seemed to be fighting to control himself. "Won't you . . . please sit down?" he asked.

Mason nodded to Paul Drake and drew up a chair.

"Now," Mason said, "time is short. Do you know Vera Martel, or did you know her during her lifetime?"

"Martel . . . Martel," Elliott said. "Why, yes. I have heard someone mention the name but I can't remember who. I think someone asked me if . . . No, I'm sorry, I can't remember."

"The police may use means to refresh your memory," Mason told him.

"I . . . Tell me, Mr. Mason, do the police think this person was killed *in* Gilman's workshop?"

"That's what they think," Mason said.

"And do they have any idea as to the exact time of death?"

"The police," Mason told him, "aren't confiding in me—and you don't seem to be doing such a good job yourself."

Elliott wet his lips with the tip of his tongue, said suddenly, "All right. I'll come clean."

"It might be advisable," Mason said.

"Yesterday morning about eight thirty I got up," Elliott said. "I can't sleep much after seven o'clock. I'd been lying there in bed and trying to remain quiet because I knew both Glamis and her mother were late sleepers."

"Go on," Mason said.

"However, I could hear someone moving around downstairs and I got the aroma of coffee. It was the aroma of coffee that did it. I tried to fight back the desire for coffee but I couldn't do it. I just had to have a cup of coffee. I knew that Glamis wasn't up. I thought her stepsister, Muriell, was downstairs because I thought I'd heard her voice. I got up and started to dress."

"All right," Mason said, "go on. What happened?"

"I walked over to the window. It was a window that was on the corner just above the dining room. I looked out of the window—I guess it would be the west window—and was standing there just idly looking out at the yard and the driveway. That big garage building which holds the cars and has the two rooms, the workshop and the darkroom, is just beyond."

"What were you doing?" Mason asked.

"As a matter of fact," Elliott said, "I remember very plainly I was just buckling the belt on my trousers. I had just finished putting them on and was getting ready to shave."

"And what happened?" Mason asked.

Elliott said, "I don't know whether it means anything, but the door of the workshop opened and Glamis came running out of the workshop. Then, after she'd taken a couple of running steps, she caught herself, stopped, turned back, pulled the door shut and then ran for all she was worth around the house."

"*Around* the house?" Mason asked.

"Well, I couldn't see her all the way around the house, but I could see her running toward the side of the building— What I mean is, she didn't come down the driveway and she didn't go in the door to the screen porch which leads into the kitchen."

"All right," Mason said, "go on. What happened after that?"

"Now, let's get this straight," Elliott said. "I'm telling

you this in strict confidence. I'm assuming that you're not going to do anything that would hurt Glamis."

"I'm trying to get at the truth at the moment," Mason said.

"You're representing Carter Gilman?"

"That's right."

"And you wouldn't sell out Glamis in order to—?"

"For heaven's sake!" Mason interrupted. "Be your age! You're sitting here swapping words when the police are probably even now headed toward this apartment. Once you get in the clutches of the police you'll talk and you'll spill everything you know."

"No, I won't," Elliott said. "They can't make me talk if I don't want to."

Mason's look was scornful. "They'll have you in front of a grand jury and they'll have you under oath. You'll tell your story, my friend, and you'll tell it right. If you lie, you'll go to prison for perjury, and if you don't lie, they'll have it out of you down to every last detail. Now tell me the rest of it."

Elliott said, "There was something about the way she acted, something . . . I just can't describe it, Mr. Mason."

"All right," Mason said. "You gathered the impression that something was going on, is that right?"

"Very much so. I thought she—she seemed to be terribly frightened."

"Go on," Mason said.

"Well, I had been trying to keep rather quiet, then I realized that she was up and presumed it would be all right to come down for breakfast, so I went into the bathroom and started shaving."

"Electric razor?"

"No, I used a safety razor and a ready-mix shaving cream."

"Go on," Mason said.

"Then I heard a peculiar creaking of boards up in the attic. That's rather an old-fashioned house and—"

"Never mind describing the house," Mason said, glancing impatiently at his wristwatch. "Tell me what happened. I've been in the house."

"Well, I heard this peculiar creaking of boards and then the next thing I heard was the sound of voices in the corridor."

"So what did you do?"

"I had lather all over my face," Elliott said, "and I wasn't very presentable. But I heard Glamis' voice and so I opened the door a crack. I was going to ask her, 'What about breakfast?' "

"And what did you see?"

"I saw Muriell standing by the open door on the attic steps and Glamis was there and . . . well, Glamis wasn't in what you would call a presentable condition."

"How was she dressed?" Mason asked.

"Well, she had on . . . I guess they were night things."

"Don't be so damned reticent," the lawyer snapped. "How was she dressed?"

"Well, she had on a filmy something on top that you could see right through and it only came down just below her hips, and . . . I don't know, I guess there were panties, but . . . well, I felt like a Peeping Tom standing there with the door open just a crack, and I didn't know what the devil to do."

"Was she facing you or away from you?"

"She was turned so she was about three quarters facing me but she wasn't looking at me, she was looking at Muriell and she seemed angry and I heard her say something about the attic and Muriell said something about her father and I gently closed the door and certainly hoped they hadn't seen me."

"Then what?" Mason asked.

"Well, I . . . frankly, I was terribly embarrassed, Mr. Mason."

"Don't be prudish," Mason said. "You'd been out with Glamis—you'd seen her in a bathing suit?"

"Certainly."

"This costume was more revealing than a bathing suit?"

"Much more. I . . . well, it was the idea of the thing, as though I'd been peeking."

"All right, what did you do?" Mason asked.

"I didn't know what to do. I finished shaving and sat around there, waiting. The aroma of coffee wasn't quite so strong and . . . well, I sat there and waited awhile for Glamis to call me."

"And then what?"

"Then . . . oh, I guess it was an hour when Glamis came and tapped on my door."

"She was fully dressed then?"

"No, she had on some sort of negligee. She was . . . well, she was presentable."

"And what happened?"

"She asked me how I'd slept and chided me for being up and fully dressed and wanted to know why I hadn't gone down and got some coffee and . . . well, we went downstairs and got some coffee and she said she'd already telephoned a service station a couple of blocks down the street and they'd promised to check my battery."

"Did you stay for breakfast?"

"Yes."

"Who cooked it?"

"Glamis. Why?"

"Where was Muriell?"

"I don't know. I didn't see her."

"Where was Nancy?"

"Asleep, I guess."

"What did you have for breakfast?"

"Some sausage and some fried eggs."

"How long did you stay there?"

"Not very long. The man from the service station came to the door and said he had put a temporary battery in the car and it was all ready to go, that they were putting my battery on a charging unit and I could have it any time that afternoon."

"So what did you do?"

"Thanked Glamis and said I was afraid I'd been a lot of nuisance and drove away."

"You went back and picked up your battery?"

"Yes."

"When?"

"Late yesterday afternoon."

"That was within two blocks of the house," Mason said. "Did you go down to see Glamis?"

"No."

"Why not?"

"I had some things I had to do and—well, I didn't have

a date with Glamis. I'd had a date with her the night before."

"You date her rather regularly?"

"If it's any of your business, yes."

"How was the farewell when you left her at the Vauxman house? Cordial?"

"Cordial."

"You kissed her?"

"Dammit, of course I kissed her!" Elliott said. "Hell, I'd been out with her half the night and I spent the rest of the night there in the house and Glamis is a sweet kid and I kissed her, and we'd been necking on the front porch before that, if it's any of your damn business, and I don't think it is."

Mason said, "It happens that it's very much my business. Your story is going to be scrutinized very carefully, and if that story is true there's a pretty damn good chance the police will decide Vera Martel was blackmailing either Glamis or her mother, that Glamis met her out in the workshop in order to pay her some blackmail money, that there was a dispute, that Glamis choked her to death and ran into the house, that Carter Gilman saw Glamis running out of the workshop, went into the workshop, found Vera Martel's body, knew what had happened, stuffed the body into the trunk of his car and drove the body out to where it was disposed of, that either Gilman or a confederate then got Vera Martel's car, which was parked near the house, and drove it off the cliff.

"A great deal will depend on the time of death. If it turns out that death could have been around eight thirty to nine o'clock you can be pretty certain Glamis is going to be dragged in as one of the defendants and you're going to be the star witness for the prosecution."

"*I* am?" Elliott exclaimed.

"To convict Glamis of first-degree murder," Mason said, watching the man closely.

Elliott said, "Don't be silly, Mr. Mason. I've told *you* this. I'm not going to tell it to anybody else."

"You just think you aren't," Mason said.

"But what . . . what do I do?"

"*I* don't know what *you* do," Mason said. "*I'm* not advising *you*. I'm representing Gilman, and if Glamis should be arrested I'll probably be representing her. I'd like to know what the true facts are. For your information, Glamis has denied that she ever knew Vera Martel or knew anything about her."

"What did she say about being out in the workshop yesterday morning?" Elliott asked.

"I didn't ask her," Mason said. And then added drily, "The police are probably asking her that now. If they aren't, they certainly will after they've talked with you."

"Can they force me to make a statement?"

"They can take you to Headquarters. If you don't talk it's going to look bad. If you do talk it's going to look terrible. They can subpoena you and take you in front of a grand jury and you'll *have* to talk."

"I don't have to talk," Elliott said.

"Then you go to jail," Mason said. "And if you lie, you go to prison for perjury."

"And if I talk, Glamis is involved in a murder case?"

"Glamis," Mason said, "is probably involved in the murder case right now. She had a chance to tell me the truth and she missed it. I don't know what's going to happen now."

"Look here," Elliott said, "suppose the police can't find me."

"They'll find you," Mason said.

"I'm not so certain they will."

"All right," Mason told him, "if you're missing and the police can't find you and the police learn that you were in that house early yesterday morning, and if the police find that Vera Martel was killed early yesterday morning, then *you're* going to be the prime suspect."

Elliott's eyes began to blink rapidly. "Well?" he asked.

"Draw your own conclusions," Mason said.

"Look here," Elliott said, "how long have I got before the police start looking for me?"

"How do I know?" Mason asked. "They're probably looking for you now."

Elliott strode over to the door, said, "Very well, gentlemen, I've told you all I know and I have things to do."

"Now look," Mason told him, "if you're planning—"

"You heard what I said, I have things to do. As far as I'm concerned, the interview is terminated."

Mason glanced at Paul Drake, nodded and the two of them walked out into the corridor.

Elliott pulled the door shut behind them.

Mason beckoned to Paul Drake and led the way to the elevator.

They were silent until they had reached the sidewalk in front of the apartment house.

"Got your car here, Paul?" Mason asked.

"Uh-huh. You came in your car?"

"That's right."

"Want me to tag him?"

Mason shook his head.

"Why not?" Drake asked. "You know what's going to happen. He's going to get the hell out of there."

"All right," Mason said. "You remember what we told him. We told him we couldn't give him any advice. We told him that if he skipped out he would become the number-one suspect in the case."

"Yes," Drake said, "you were highly ethical, but if I were in Hartley Elliott's shoes and if I were in love with Glamis, I think I'd suddenly have some business that took me out of the country."

"And you'd like to follow him to find out where he goes?"

"Well, it might help," Drake said.

"Help whom?" Mason asked.

Drake thought that over for a moment, then grinned and said, "Okay, I get you, Perry. Do you want me to follow you to the office?"

"Keep me in sight all the way," Mason said.

CHAPTER ELEVEN

THE PRELIMINARY HEARING in the Case of the People of the State of California versus Carter Gilman started out in a routine manner as a conventional preliminary hearing.

However, veteran courtroom attachés noticed that the deputy district attorney, Edwardo Marcus Deering, was much more careful with his evidence and was laying a more firm foundation for an order binding the defendant over than would have been the case if the renowned Perry Mason had not been representing the defendant.

Deering, having confided to associates that this time he was going to establish such an ironclad case that not even Perry Mason could find a loophole in it, called the state police officer who had found Vera Martel's body.

The officer described the tracks indicating a car had left the road, his subsequent inspection of the premises, his finding the body in the car wedged behind the steering wheel. He testified that the automatic gearshift of the car was in the drive position but that, in his opinion as an expert, the car had been barely crawling when it moved to the outside of the curve and plunged down the grade.

The tracks were not those of a skidding car trying to make a curve and then lunging out of control, but between the shoulder of the pavement and the end of the road where there was a few feet of dirt, the tracks showed very plainly that the automobile had been pointed directly at the curve and had gone over, not at a tangent as would have been the case with a speeding car, but in a direct line which would have been the case only if the car had been deliberately pointed at the precipice.

Moreover, rocks which had been dislodged by the automobile as it went over the cliff indicated that the initial velocity of the car had been such as to displace the rocks only a very short distance. There was no indication of speed.

The officer introduced photographs of the car, of the body, and of the dislodged rocks.

Mason gave the testimony of the witness thoughtful attention, but when he was invited to cross-examine, smiled and said, "No questions, Your Honor."

Judge Boris Alvord excused the witness and regarded Perry Mason with thoughtful speculation.

"May I ask if the defense intends to make any showing in this case?" he asked.

"We don't know yet, Your Honor."

"Do you know whether you will resist an order binding the defendant over?"

"Yes, Your Honor, we will resist it."

"Very well," Judge Alvord said to the prosecutor, "call your next witness."

The next witness was an autopsy surgeon who testified to various broken bones and internal injuries.

"Can you give your opinion as to the cause of death?" Deering asked.

Judge Alvord glanced at Mason, expecting an objection. Mason sat tight and said nothing.

"In my opinion," the autopsy surgeon said, "death was due to manual strangulation. The broken bones and internal injuries were post-mortem and were incurred, I would say, at least two hours after death."

"Can you give an approximate time of death?" Deering asked.

"I would say that death occurred some time between seven thirty A.M. and eleven thirty A.M. of the day preceding that on which the body was discovered."

"Cross-examine," Deering said to Perry Mason.

"No questions," Mason said.

The deputy coroner called to the stand identified the personal property which had been in the purse of Vera Martel. The purse had been taken from the wrecked automobile.

"With particular reference to this key container containing several keys," Deering asked, "did you mark this key container in any way for identification?"

"I did."

"Does that have your identifying mark on it?"

"It does."

"Is this the key container which was taken from Vera Martel's automobile?"

"It is."

"Cross-examine," Deering said to Mason.

Mason shook his head. "No questions."

"Call Jonathan Blair," Deering said.

Jonathan Blair qualified himself as a technical criminological expert for the sheriff's office.

"Did you make a microscopic examination of the clothing and of the body of Vera Martel?" Deering asked.

"I did."

"Specifically, what did you find in the way of unusual foreign bodies?"

"I found bits of sawdust adhering to the skirt, to the top of one of the stockings and in both of the shoes."

"Can you describe this sawdust?"

"The sawdust," Blair said, "came from various types of wood. There was satinwood, sandalwood, a rare type of mahogany, myrtlewood and fragments of mahogany which had been stained a deep red."

"Was this a varnish or oil?" Deering asked.

"It was neither. It was a dye which had been made to impregnate the wood."

"Did you make any attempt to trace this particular wood?"

"I did. I was given samples of mahogany which had been similarly treated by a dealer named Carlos Barbara. I compared samples of wood which he gave me with some of the particles of sawdust and was able to make a spectroscopic analysis showing that the dye used in both specimens was identical."

"Cross-examine," Deering said.

Mason shook his head. "No questions on cross-examination, Your Honor."

Deering said, "Call Carlos Barbara."

Barbara testified that he dealt in rare woods for cabinetworkers, that he had recently evolved the process by which a certain chemical dye which he had invented could be utilized to stain a certain type of mahogany. The process was, he said, secret. The wood was seasoned in a certain manner and at a certain time the dye was introduced under pressure. It was a process that no other dealer had duplicated and he had had it perfected on a commercial basis for less than three months.

Deering asked him if his books indicated persons to whom that mahogany had been sold and Barbara stated that he had not sold any of the mahogany, that he had given three people samples to use for testing. Those three people had been three of his good customers, three persons whom he knew were interested in a new type of wood.

"Was the defendant one of those persons?" Deering asked.

"That's right. I gave Mr. Gilman a sample."

Deering said, "I show you a piece of wood and ask you if that is one of the pieces of wood you gave Mr. Gilman."

"That is part of it, yes. It has been sawed approximately in two pieces. That is about half of the piece I gave Mr. Gilman."

"We ask that this be marked for identification," Deering said.

"No objection," Mason said. "In fact, if you will state that this piece of wood was found in Mr. Gilman's woodworking shop I will be willing to stipulate that such is the case and it may be received in evidence."

"I will so state," Deering said, his manner somewhat puzzled.

"Then I will so stipulate," Mason said.

Judge Alvord looked at Mason as though about to say something, then changed his mind and said, "Very well. The wood will be received in evidence with that stipulation. Proceed."

"I have no further questions, Your Honor."

"No cross-examination," Mason said.

"I now wish to call Warren Lawton," Deering said.

Lawton qualified himself as a technical expert with the Los Angeles Police Department.

"I will ask you if you examined sawdust which had adhered to the skirt of Vera Martel and sawdust which was found in her shoes and on the top of one stocking."

"I was present when the sawdust was recovered by vacuum cleaner from the articles of clothing mentioned."

"Was any of that sawdust composed of particles of this same wood containing this same dye which has been introduced in evidence as People's Exhibit G?"

"They were."

"Where were they found?"

"In the right shoe near the heel, near the top of the right stocking and on the skirt, both the right and the left sides."

"Did you make any examination of an automobile registered in the name of Carter Gilman?"

"I did."

"Did you find anything significant in the trunk of that automobile?"

"I did."

"What was it?"

"Some of the same type of sawdust coming from this board, Exhibit G; some fibers which, in my opinion, came from the skirt worn by Vera Martel at the time of her death—or at least the skirt she had on when her body was found—and several hairs which, in my opinion, are exactly identical with hairs from the head of Vera Martel."

"Did you find anything else in the car which you considered significant?"

"I did."

"What was it?"

"A rather large lump of blue modeling clay."

"Can you describe this modeling clay?"

"It is a clay about the consistency of putty. It is colored a deep blue, and it retains its plasticity; that is, it doesn't become dry and hard as other clay but remains soft and pliable."

"Cross-examine," Deering said.

Mason arose to face the witness. "You found this type of sawdust in the defendant's workshop?"

"Yes."

"That type of sawdust would adhere to a person's clothes?"

"Some of it would under proper circumstances, yes."

"If Vera Martel had been in that workshop, lying on the floor, do you feel that some of the sawdust would have adhered to her clothing?"

"I feel quite certain it would have."

"And if her body had been placed in the automobile you think some of that sawdust might have become loosened?"

"I think there is no question but what it would, yes."

"There's nothing about this sawdust, no peculiarity which gives it a particular affinity for the type of clothing worn by Vera Martel?"

"No, sir."

"It would adhere to the defendant's clothing?"

"Yes, sir."

"Then, by the same sign, if the defendant had been working in his workshop and wearing, let us say, a sports coat at the time, this sawdust would have adhered to the sleeves of the defendant's coat?"

"It could have."

"And, if some of this sawdust was on the sports coat of the defendant and the defendant had opened the trunk of his automobile to put something in or get something out, it is quite possible that particles of this sawdust would have dropped from the coat sleeves of the defendant?"

"That is possible."

"Thank you," Mason said. "No further questions."

"Call Maurice Fellows," Deering said, with the air of a card player who is about to trump an opponent's ace.

Fellows, an older man with bushy eyebrows, heavy caliper lines around his mouth and a fringe of somewhat unkempt hair around his temples and the back of his head, took the stand and gave his occupation as a person who made keys.

"Are you acquainted with the defendant?" Deering asked.

"I've seen him."

"When did you see him?"

"On the afternoon of the thirteenth."

"That was last Tuesday afternoon?"

"Yes, sir."

"Did you have any business transactions with him?"

"Yes, sir."

"Generally, what did those transactions consist of?"

Fellows said, "The defendant brought me in a lump of modeling clay. In it were the impressions of five keys. He wanted keys made to fit those impressions. I told him we didn't ordinarily do that work and it would be quite a job, that we'd have to charge extra, that I'd have to make a master pattern and . . ."

"And what did he say?"

"He said to go ahead, never mind the expense, to get the keys for him just as soon as possible."

"What did you do?"

"I made the keys."

"Now, how did you make those keys?"

"I first made a master pattern to use in making duplicates."

"Did you retain those master patterns?"

"I did."

"Do you have them with you?"

"I do."

"I ask that they be introduced in evidence," Deering said.

"No objection," Mason said.

"Now, Mr. Fellows, I am handing you a key container which has already been introduced in evidence as having been found in the purse of Vera Martel, the decedent, and ask you as an expert key man if these patterns which you have match any of the keys found in this key container."

"They do," the witness said.

"All of them?"

"All of them."

"You may cross-examine," Deering said, with an air of sudden swift triumph.

"No questions at this time," Mason said.

Judge Alvord glanced at the clock and said, "Well, gentlemen, it's five minutes before the noon hour. I think we had better take an adjournment before you call any more witnesses—or do you have any more, Mr. Prosecutor?"

"I think we have a couple," Deering said.

"Very well. The court will take an adjournment until one thirty this afternoon. The defendant is remanded to custody."

Judge Alvord left the bench.

Mason arose, nodded to the officer, said, "Could you bring Mr. Gilman back here about twenty minutes past one, Officer? I want to have a talk with him before court convenes."

"I'll have him here," the officer said.

"All right," Mason said to Gilman, "think it over. You're going to have to tell me the truth now."

Mason picked up his brief case, nodded to Della Street and they were joined by Paul Drake as they left the courtroom.

"Lunch?" Drake asked.

"A light lunch," Mason said. "Just a few groceries to keep us going."

"That key business puts the noose right around your client's neck," Paul Drake said lugubriously.

Mason said nothing.

"The fact they brought that out at a preliminary examination shows they're afraid of you, however. Ordinarily they'd have saved that for the main trial."

"Except that by putting it in the record now," Mason said, "they can use it later on in case this key man can't be found."

Drake said, "Well, this is once they have you lashed to the mast, Perry. It's a wonder Hamilton Burger hasn't moved in for the kill."

"Probably because it's too open and shut," Mason said. "The district attorney wouldn't come into court personally on a case that's as open and shut as this."

"I'll bet you even money he's there this afternoon to conduct the examination himself," Paul Drake said. "He's in need of a personal triumph to satisfy his ego."

Mason said, "The guy doesn't look like a murderer, and yet . . ."

"For my money, he did the job," Drake said. "He did it to protect someone he loved, but he did it."

They went to their favorite restaurant near the Hall of Justice where there was a small private dining room which a friendly proprietor kept in reserve for Perry Mason on court days.

Midway through the light lunch the waiter appeared with a telephone. "A call for Mr. Drake," he said.

He plugged the phone in, Drake picked up the instrument, said, "Okay, this is Paul Drake. . . . Who? . . . Okay, put her on."

Drake said, "Hello," listened for a few moments, then said, "Okay. I guess there's nothing we can do. Just keep on the job. I'm glad we picked up the information."

Drake pushed back the instrument, said, "I hate to bring you more bad news, Perry."

"Can it get any worse?" Mason asked.

"The police have picked up Hartley Elliott. They're holding him as a material witness. They've had him for more than six hours but have kept him under cover. They're planning to put him on this afternoon as a surprise witness. They want to catch you flat-footed and figured that your cross-examination isn't going to help the situation any if they take you by surprise.

"Then they'll give Elliott every opportunity to skip out before the trial if he wants to and they'll read the testimony of Elliott at the preliminary hearing into the record. That will make it even more deadly.

"They've been planning that carefully as prosecution strategy. They had Elliott spotted where he was living under an assumed name in a motel and have had him under surveillance for a couple of days. They picked him up early this morning in a surprise move and are planning to steal a march on you.

"You know what that means. Hamilton Burger himself will be in the courtroom this afternoon, ready to jerk the rug out from under you, and while they've got you floundering they'll make Elliott admit that he saw Glamis running from the workshop. The theory is that Gilman, sitting at the breakfast table, also saw her running and went out to find out what it was all about, either encountered Vera Martel and strangled her or found that Glamis had done the job and is covering up for Glamis.

"Then they'll call the grand jury in session, indict Glamis, try her jointly with Carter Gilman and have you where you can't squirm out."

Mason said, "Glamis insists she was in bed until she heard Muriell moving around upstairs."

"Uh-huh," Drake said, "that's what she insists, but by the time your client tells you the real truth you'll find you have a bear by the tail."

Mason pushed back his chair from the table. "Well," he said, "let's go up to the scene of the massacre and watch Hamilton Burger move in for the kill."

CHAPTER TWELVE

PROMPTLY at one twenty the officer brought Carter Gilman into court.

Mason glanced over his shoulder at the spectators who were already filling up the benches in the courtroom, put his arm along the back of the chair in which Gilman was sitting, kept his manner casual and said in a low voice, "All right, tell me the story, the true story."

Mason turned as though about to pick up a paper, then again leaned toward Gilman. "All right, let me have it."

Gilman said, "I'm not going to betray the person I'm trying to protect."

Mason said, "I can't protect anyone unless I know the facts—all of them."

"Then you'd betray me."

"Not you. You're my client."

"Then you'd betray the person I'm trying to protect, in order to save my life."

Mason studied the man. "I might do just that."

"That's what I'm afraid of. I'll never tell any living soul what I saw."

"All right," Mason said. "You're going to get a jolt within a few minutes."

"What do you mean?"

"I mean the police have Hartley Elliott in custody. He

was in the bedroom over the dining room. He saw Glamis when she ran out of the workshop."

Had Mason hit Gilman in the stomach the man couldn't have shown greater surprise and dismay. "He—he *saw* her."

"That's right."

"How do you know?"

"He told me."

Gilman heaved a deep sigh. "Of all the luck! He would have had to be looking out that window."

"Was it Glamis?" Mason asked.

"Yes. First Vera Martel walked up the driveway and entered the darkroom. I saw her. I made an excuse to get Muriell out in the kitchen so I could go out and investigate. Then in the few minutes that necessarily elapsed . . . well, I don't know what happened. I looked out of the window and Glamis came running out of the workshop.

"It seemed Muriell never would quit popping in and out of that kitchen door. I had to wait until I was certain she was engaged in the cooking before I—"

The bailiff banged his gavel. "Everybody rise!"

The occupants of the courtroom got to their feet as Judge Alvord came in and took his place on the bench.

A side door opened and Hamilton Burger came into the courtroom to seat himself beside Edwardo Deering.

Judge Alvord seemed mildly surprised. "Am I to understand the district attorney is appearing in this case personally?" he asked.

"Yes, Your Honor," Hamilton Burger said, and, turning, nodded coolly to Perry Mason.

"Very well," Judge Alvord said. "Call your next witness."

Deering said, "I call Hartley Grove Elliott."

Burger arose to address the Court. "May the Court please," he said, "Hartley Elliott is not only a hostile witness, I may state to the Court that we have been forced to bring him to court as a material witness who has been picked up and held in custody. Mr. Elliott not only endeavored to avoid a subpoena but was living in a motel under an assumed name and endeavoring to conceal his whereabouts from the authorities."

"The Court will permit leading questions," Judge Alvord ruled, "if the hostility of the witness becomes apparent. However, you can examine him in the regular manner until it becomes apparent that leading questions are required."

The door from the witness room opened and a uniformed officer escorted Hartley Elliott into the courtroom.

Judge Alvord, watching Elliott curiously, said, "Raise your right hand and be sworn."

Elliott raised his right hand, was sworn and took the witness stand.

"I'm directing your attention to the morning of Tuesday, the thirteenth of this month," Hamilton Burger said, conducting the examination personally.

"Yes, sir," Elliott said.

"Where were you on that morning?"

"I was at the home of the defendant, Carter Gilman, at 6231 Vauxman Avenue."

"Were you a guest in that home?"

"I was."

"What time did you arrive there?"

"Do you want to know when I first arrived there?"

"That is what the question calls for."

"About two or two thirty in the morning, I would presume."

"And what did you do?"

"I escorted Glamis Barlow to the house. We sat on the porch for a while, then she invited me in for a drink."

"And then?" Hamilton Burger asked.

"Then I said good night and went out to start my car. She came to stand in the doorway and see me off. I had inadvertently left the ignition on. My battery had evidently been run down. When I tried to start the car the self-starter wouldn't work."

"Then what happened?"

"Miss Barlow suggested that I stay there in the house until morning, when I could get another battery put in my car and in the meantime have my own battery charged at a nearby service station."

"Was that service station open at that hour of the morning?"

"Not when I tried to start the car, no. It opened at eight o'clock in the morning."

"All right," Hamilton Burger said. "What did you do then?"

"I went to bed."

"Now then," Hamilton Burger said, "I want to have the Court understand exactly where you were sleeping. Can you describe the bedroom?"

"It was on the northwest corner of the house."

"That was toward the back of the house?"

"Yes."

"From your room could you see the garage in back of the house?"

"Yes."

"Are you familiar with the location of the darkroom used by Mrs. Gilman?"

"Yes."

"And you are also familiar with the woodworking shop used by the defendant in this case, Carter Gilman?"

"Yes."

"I refer you to People's Exhibit B, a sketch of the floor plan of the house showing the location of the driveway, the garage, the workshop and the darkroom. Do you orient yourself on that diagram?"

"Yes."

"Will you kindly point out to the Court exactly where your bedroom was located?"

"It was this bedroom on the second floor."

"And that is directly over the dining room?"

"I believe so, yes."

"Now then, I am going to ask you, when did you next see Glamis Barlow after you had said good night to her at an early hour in the morning on the thirteenth? When was the very next time you saw her?"

"I—I refuse to answer."

"On what ground?"

"I simply refuse to answer."

Hamilton Burger looked at Judge Alvord.

Judge Alvord said, "The witness will answer unless there is something in the question that would tend to incriminate or degrade him, in which event he can place his refusal to answer on those grounds and the Court will then pass upon the refusal."

"I refuse to answer."

"If you simply refuse to answer," Judge Alvord said, "you are going to be held in contempt of this court."

"I simply refuse to answer. I am not going to permit anything I may have seen to be used to crucify an innocent person."

Hamilton Burger frowned.

"Very well," Judge Alvord said. "If you refuse to answer the Court is going to hold you in contempt, and I may assure you, Mr. Elliott, that this contempt is not going to be a light sentence. This is a continuing matter. This is a murder case. Your evidence may be vital."

"I refuse to answer."

Hamilton Burger said, "If the Court please, I feel that the Court should use sufficient pressure to get an answer from this witness. Here we have a hostile witness who has evidence which may have a great bearing upon the solution of this case. It may furnish evidence not only as to motivation, but it may indicate the necessity of having two defendants jointly charged with this murder. The answer of this witness is of very great importance. I can assure the Court that, in view of the attitude of this witness, in view of the fact that the witness has already endeavored to conceal himself, there is every possibility that the witness will not be available at the time of trial in the Superior Court unless he is held in custody as a material witness. Even then, it is impossible to anticipate what his testimony may be after he has had an opportunity to think it over and to be coached by interested parties.

"It is vital to the case of the People that this witness be forced to answer this question here and now."

Judge Alvord said, "Mr. Elliott, I am going to warn you

that unless you answer this question you are going to be committed to jail for contempt of court and you are going to stay in jail until you do answer the question or until you show some legal grounds why the question should not be answered."

"I refuse to answer."

"Very well," Judge Alvord said, "it is the judgment of this Court that you forthwith be committed to the sheriff of this county, that you be confined in the county jail for contempt of this court and that you be held in the county jail until such time as you either answer this question or show legal cause why you should not answer it."

Hartley Elliott stood up, folded his arms, regarded the judge with steady, steely eyes and said, "I refuse to answer."

Judge Alvord nodded to the officer.

The officer came forward, took Elliott's arm and escorted him from the courtroom.

Hamilton Burger turned dramatically. "I call Paul Drake to the stand," he said. "Paul Drake is here in the courtroom. Come forward and be sworn, Mr. Drake."

Drake glanced in dismay at Perry Mason.

"Come forward and be sworn, Mr. Drake," Judge Alvord ordered.

Drake came forward, was sworn and took the stand.

"You are a private detective?"

"Yes, sir."

"Licensed as such?"

"Yes, sir."

"And were so licensed on the fourteenth day of this month?"

"Yes, sir."

"Are you acquainted with Hartley Elliott, the witness who was just on the stand?"

"Yes, sir."

"I am going to ask you if, on the fourteenth day of this month, in the apartment of Hartley Elliott, number 6-B at the Rossiter Apartments on Blendon Street in this city, you and Perry Mason did not have a conversation with Hartley Elliott. Now, you can answer that question yes or no."

Drake hesitated, finally said reluctantly, "Yes."

"I am going to ask you," Hamilton Burger said, "if at that conversation and in the presence of Perry Mason as attorney for the defense you did not ask Hartley Elliott what had happened on the morning of the thirteenth and if Hartley Elliott didn't then and there tell you that he had seen Glamis Barlow at about eight thirty on the morning of the thirteenth, dash from the door of the workshop, previously referred to in this testimony and shown on the diagram, People's Exhibit B, and run around the corner of the house."

Mason got to his feet. "Just a moment, if the Court please," he said. "I object to the question on the ground that it calls for hearsay testimony."

"It is by way of impeachment," Hamilton Burger said.

"There is nothing to impeach," Mason said. "Even if Hartley Elliott had testified that he *hadn't* seen Glamis Barlow on the morning of the thirteenth it would still be an improper question. An attorney cannot impeach his own witness."

"He can if he shows surprise at the answer of the witness," Hamilton Burger said.

"Are you prepared to state that you were surprised?"

Mason asked. "Hadn't Hartley Elliott told you before you ever put him on the stand that he would refuse to answer any question as to what had happened on the morning of the thirteenth?"

Hamilton Burger's countenance showed that the shot had told.

"I am waiting to see if you can assure the Court such is the fact," Mason said.

"That is immaterial," Hamilton Burger blurted.

"No, it isn't immaterial," Mason said. "You can't impeach your own witness unless you can show surprise. You can't impeach any witness except by showing that at some time he has made a statement contrary to the testimony he has given, and even then the testimony by way of impeachment cannot be considered as evidence of the facts stated but only as evidence that the witness has made a contradictory statement at some time and that his veracity is thereby brought into question."

"I think that is the law," Judge Alvord said.

Hamilton Burger's face reddened. "Your Honor," he said, "the prosecution doesn't want to be boxed in by a lot of technicalities. The prosecution has reason to believe that Perry Mason and Paul Drake, his detective, had a conversation with Hartley Elliott on the fourteenth, that as a result of that conversation Hartley Elliott hurriedly left his apartment shortly before the police arrived, that he went to a motel where he registered under an assumed name and tried to keep out of circulation so that he could not be found and couldn't be questioned by the police or subpoenaed as a witness in this case.

"Now then, if the Court please, we believe that Hartley Elliott actually saw Glamis Barlow run from the workshop and that he told Paul Drake and Perry Mason that, and I think it is a reasonable inference that his disappearance was connected with the conversation he had with those two gentlemen."

Judge Alvord glanced at Perry Mason.

Perry Mason said, "That's a theory the prosecutor has, Your Honor, but I still submit that he can't prove any fact in this case against the defendant by hearsay testimony. He has to produce some direct testimony if he wants to show motivation for the murder of Vera Martel, which apparently he is trying to show. He has to show that by direct evidence, not by what some witness may have told someone. If he wants to impeach a witness he has to be governed by the rules of impeachment."

"And you object to the question?" Judge Alvord asked.

"We object to it on the ground that it is incompetent, irrelevant and immaterial, that it calls for hearsay evidence, that it is an attempt by the prosecutor to impeach his own witness."

"The objection is sustained," Judge Alvord said.

Hamilton Burger, his face flushed, snapped, "That's all, Mr. Drake. You may step down from the stand. You may also remember that you are licensed as a detective and that that license is coming up for renewal."

"If the Court please," Mason said, "we object to the prosecutor threatening the witness and we respectfully submit that it is no breach of ethics to fail to answer a question which the Court has ruled calls for inadmissible testimony. In fact, if the witness had volunteered to answer the question after the objection was sustained, he would have been in contempt of court."

Judge Alvord suppressed a smile. "Very well," he said.

"The district attorney is admonished not to attempt to intimidate witnesses. The Court has ruled the question called for an answer which would have been inadmissible, the objection to the question was sustained. The witness would have been out of order if he had volunteered the information. The rebuke is uncalled for, Mr. District Attorney.

"Call your next witness."

Hamilton Burger, his face flushed with anger, said, "If the Court please, I'm going to get at this another way. Call Glamis Barlow to the stand."

Judge Alvord stroked his chin reflectively. "Miss Barlow is in court?" he asked.

"I have had her subpoenaed, and since she is a material witness and I am afraid she may leave the jurisdiction of the court I arranged to have her taken into custody a few hours ago."

"I don't know just what you are trying to accomplish, Mr. District Attorney," Judge Alvord said. "This Court is conducting a preliminary hearing. The only purpose of a preliminary hearing is to show, first, that a crime has been committed; second, that there is probable cause to believe the defendant is connected with the perpetration of the crime. The function of this Court is not to act as a grand jury."

"I understand that, Your Honor," Hamilton Burger said coldly.

"Now, I also realize," Judge Alvord went on, "that under the law of this state, where a person has been called as a witness at a preliminary hearing and has either been cross-examined by the defense, or counsel for the defense has had an opportunity to cross-examine that witness, if anything should happen that at the trial of the case the witness is unavailable, either party can read the testimony of that witness into evidence; that is, the testimony of the witness as given at the preliminary examination."

"Yes, Your Honor."

"Now, therefore," Judge Alvord went on, "it sometimes happens that a district attorney who has a witness who can give important testmony in a case and who he fears may have either died or removed from the jurisdiction of the court by the time the case is called for trial in the Superior Court, can produce a witness at a preliminary hearing and thereby forestall difficulties which may arise if the witness is not available at the time of the trial."

"Yes, Your Honor," Hamilton Burger said coldly.

Judge Alvord showed his exasperation. "I do not wish to superimpose my judgment upon that of the prosecution in this case," he said. "Nor, on the other hand, do I propose to have this Court used to usurp the functions of a grand jury. I simply tried to make my observations in a manner friendly to both counsel, yet bearing in mind that it is the object of this Court to see that justice is done.

"Now, Mr. Prosecutor, you have established a prima-facie case. It is a well-known fact that once that has happened Courts usually bind the defendant over for trial, that even if the defense is able to put on evidence which raises a question as to the accuracy of the evidence introduced by the prosecution, the Court in a preliminary hearing will not take the responsibility of weighing that evidence or resolving the conflict in that evidence but will bind the defendant over for trial.

"The Court feels that it is, therefore, entitled to ask the prosecutor why the prosecution is so anxious to continue with these witnesses and a line of testimony which apparently is merely cumulative."

"The prosecution desires to do so because it feels it is good policy to do so," Hamilton Burger said. "The prosecution is dealing with a resourceful, tricky trial attorney who is accustomed to capitalize upon the dramatic in order to upset the conventions of courtroom precedent. The prosecution, therefore, insists that it have the right to put on its case as it sees fit and that the Court does not restrain the prosecution from calling witnesses."

"Very well," Judge Alvord said, his manner indicating that he was becoming progressively more angry, "the Court is not going to restrain the rights of the prosecution to put on witnesses. On the other hand, this is a court of justice and the Court does not intend to be used as a grand jury, nor does it intend to see any defendant deprived of his or her rights.

"Now then, Mr. District Attorney, you want to call Glamis Barlow to the stand. It is quite apparent that before this case is finished there is every possibility Glamis Barlow will be joined as a codefendant in a trial in the Superior Court. The Court does not propose to have Miss Barlow called as a witness simply in order to entrap her into a situation where she may have forfeited any of her constitutional rights.

"You want to call Miss Barlow as a witness. Go ahead and call her."

"Glamis Barlow," Hamilton Burger said in an unnecessarily loud voice.

An officer opened the door of the witness room and escorted Glamis Barlow to the stand.

"Now, just a moment," Judge Alvord said, after the

witness had taken the oath. "Miss Barlow, you are being called as a witness in this case by the prosecution. The Court feels it is only fair to you to warn you that testimony has been received indicating a strong possibility that you may be implicated in the murder which is the subject of this investigation, or that an attempt may be made to implicate you as a defendant.

"The Court advises you that you are not called upon to answer any question which, in your opinion, may tend to incriminate you. The prosecution does not have any right to call you as a witness in a case in which you are the defendant. While you are not formally a defendant in this case, you may later on become one. The Court wants you to understand your situation and the Court further advises you that if you wish to confer with counsel at any time the Court is going to give you the opportunity to do so. Do you understand?"

"Yes, Your Honor," Glamis Barlow said.

"And," Judge Alvord went on, "anything you may say now, any answer you may give to questions now asked you can be used against you at any time. Do you so understand?"

"Yes, Your Honor."

"The Court has committed one witness for contempt for failing to answer a question. This Court will, however, be far more charitable with a witness who is obviously being called in an attempt to lay the foundation for a later prosecution, and where the idea seems to be to surprise her into making a statement before she has the advice of counsel."

"I resent the Court's remarks," Hamilton Burger said. "I feel they are uncalled for."

Judge Alvord said, "I do not agree. I advise this witness that if she wishes to refuse to answer any question there will be no contempt until after she has been given an opportunity to confer with counsel of her own choosing in order to see if she cares to answer such question.

"You may proceed, Mr. District Attorney."

Hamilton Burger turned to the witness savagely. "Are you acquainted with the decedent, Vera M. Martel, or were you acquainted with her during her lifetime?"

"Objected to, if the Court please," Mason said. "Incompetent, irrelevant and immaterial."

The Court said, "I will overrule the objection to this question."

"I did not know Vera M. Martel," Glamis Barlow said.

"I will direct your attention to the morning of the thirteenth of this month and ask you if, between the hour of eight and eight thirty, you were at your residence at 6231 Vauxman Avenue?"

"I was."

"Between those times, or at any other time during the morning, did you have occasion to go to the workshop of the defendant, Carter Gilman? Now, by that workshop I am referring to this workshop indicated on the diagram, People's Exhibit B. I want to be sure there is no misunderstanding. I am indicating on the diagram the workshop in question. Can you orient yourself according to this diagram, Miss Barlow?"

"I can."

"Did you go to that workshop?"

"Just a minute," Perry Mason said. "That is objected to as incompetent, irrelevant and immaterial. It is further objected to on the ground that the question is leading and suggestive, that it is an attempt on the part of counsel to cross-examine his own witness, that very apparently this question is designed for the purpose of trapping the witness into a position where she will be forced to be a witness against herself by the time the case comes to trial in the Superior Court; that the constitutional rights of the witness are being detoured by a technique which is not a legitimate part of the preliminary hearing in this case."

"The Court is inclined to sustain that objection," Judge Alvord said.

"If the Court please," Hamilton Burger said angrily, "this witness has been advised of her constitutional rights. I am asking her now if she went to that particular room on that particular date at that particular time, and I have a right to an answer to that question. The witness is not charged with any crime as yet."

"Will you state that it is not your intention to charge her with a crime as soon as this preliminary hearing is finished?" Judge Alvord asked.

"I will make no statement whatever to Court or counsel in regard to the intentions of the prosecution. I am at the moment calling a witness who, I believe, is familiar with certain facts in this case. I want to have her testimony made a part of this record. I am within my rights, I am not abusing the process of the Court, and I insist that the witness answer that question."

"I *want* to answer that question," Glamis Barlow shouted. "I wasn't anywhere near that room."

Hamilton Burger's face twisted into a triumphant grin. "Let's not misunderstand each other, Miss Barlow," he said suavely. "This diagram, People's Exhibit B, shows the ground-floor plan of the house at 6231 Vauxman Avenue in this city as it existed on the thirteenth day of this month, and in the question that I asked you I indicated the workshop shown on that diagram—and so that there can be no misunderstanding about it I will now ask you to write your name on the diagram indicating the room in question which you said you did not visit on the morning of the thirteenth between the hours of eight and eight thirty A.M."

"If the Court please," Mason said, "I object on the ground that this is an attempt to entrap the witness and to deprive her of her constitutional rights."

Glamis Barlow did not wait for a ruling by the Court but walked up to the diagram which had been spread out on the court blackboard.

"Just a minute, Miss Barlow," Judge Alvord said, "do you understand that question?"

"I certainly do."

"Do you wish to write your name upon the portion of the diagram which is indicated in the question?"

"I do."

"Do you realize that by so doing you are giving testimony under oath as a witness in a case wherein it is quite possible you may be a codefendant by the time the case comes to trial in the Superior Court?"

"I don't care where it is tried," Glamis Barlow said. "I wasn't anywhere near that room any time during the morning of the thirteenth. I slept until nearly ten o'clock and outside of leaving my room to go in the hallway and talk with Muriell Gilman I didn't go anywhere before at least nine thirty. Then I dressed and had breakfast and left the house and didn't go anywhere near that workroom."

"Very well," Judge Alvord said. "The Court is satisfied that you have been advised as to your constitutional rights. The Court doesn't particularly approve of this procedure but I am satisfied there is no law against it. I will state to the witness, however, that even if she did not claim the constitutional privilege of refusing to incriminate herself the Court would be inclined to sustain this objection, were it not for the attitude of the witness. Go ahead and write your name on that diagram if that is what you wish to do."

Glamis Barlow wrote her name in a firm hand on the diagram.

Hamilton Burger said gloatingly, "Now you have written your name on a section of the diagram which is labeled 'Workroom of Defendant' and is indicated by a rectangle with measurements to scale included in a larger rectangle labeled 'Garage, Darkroom and Workshop.' Is that correct?"

"That is correct."

"And you have no difficulty in orienting yourself as to that diagram and what is indicated thereby?"

"None whatever."

"When you say that you did not go into that room, you mean the workroom maintained by the defendant as a woodworking room in the southern portion of a house which is in back of the building at 6231 Vauxman Avenue, and which house or structure includes a woodworking shop on the south, a darkroom maintained by your mother, Nancy Gilman, immediately adjacent thereto, and is, in turn, adjoined on the north by a garage having room for three cars. Is that correct?"

"That is correct."

"Cross-examine," Hamilton Burger said triumphantly to Perry Mason.

"No questions," Mason said.

"Call your next witness," Judge Alvord announced.

"Call Mrs. Lamay C. Kirk," Hamilton Burger said.

The door of the witness room was opened and a rather plump, pleasant-faced woman in the early forties was escorted into the courtroom. She walked gracefully with a free, swinging motion of hips and shoulders, held up her right hand, was sworn, and took the witness stand.

"Where do you reside, Mrs. Kirk?" Hamilton Burger asked.

"6227 Vauxman Avenue."

"Now, that is where, with reference to the house occupied by the defendant, Carter Gilman?"

"It is directly south of that house."

"Are there any houses between you and the Gilman house?"

"No, sir."

"Is there a driveway?"

"No, sir. There is a hedge which extends partway between the two houses, but the driveway to the Gilman house is on the north of their house and the driveway of our house is to the south."

"I will ask you if you have occasion to remember the thirteenth of this month at an hour between eight and eight thirty in the morning."

"I do."

"What were you doing at that time?"

"I was sitting in a breakfast nook in my house."

"Where is that breakfast nook?"

"It is on the northwest corner of the house."

"And looking to the north from the windows of that house what do you see?"

"Well, we see a portion of our yard, a portion of the backyard of the Gilman house, a part of the back of the Gilman house; that is, the door to the screened porch on the back of the Gilman house, and we see the house which is used by the Gilmans as a garage and combination workshop and darkroom."

"Are you familiar with that house?"

"I see it almost every day."

"Are you acquainted with Glamis Barlow?"

"I am."

"How long have you known her?"

"Ever since we lived on Vauxman Avenue."

"How long has that been?"

"About two years."

"Have you talked with Glamis Barlow?"

"Many times."

"Did you see Glamis Barlow on the morning of the thirteenth, between the hours of eight and eight thirty A.M.?"

"I object, if the Court please," Mason said, "on the ground that the question is leading and suggestive, on the further ground that it is incompetent, irrelevant and immaterial, and that, at most, it is an attempt on the part of the prosecution to impeach its own witness, Glamis Barlow."

"We're not trying to impeach anyone," Hamilton Burger said, "we're trying to establish the facts in this case."

"I would like to ask what possible connection the appearance of Glamis Barlow in this case might have with the guilt or innocence of the defendant, Carter Gilman," Mason said.

"I'll be glad to answer that question," Hamilton Burger snapped. "Vera Martel was engaged in a business transaction which directly affected Glamis Barlow. We don't know the exact nature of that business but we can prove, at least by inference, that Glamis Barlow met Vera Martel on the morning of the thirteenth and that this defendant, seated in the dining room of his home, witnessed that meeting and, hurriedly excusing himself, went to the workshop in order to talk with Vera Martel; that while the defendant was in that workshop and while Glamis Barlow was also present, the defendant strangled Vera Martel, loaded her body in the trunk of his automobile and hurriedly left the house, leaving unfinished a portion of his breakfast; that the defendant thereupon located the automobile of Vera Martel and, with the assistance of Glamis Barlow as his accomplice, drove the Martel car to the point where the body was disposed of. The defendant attempted to make the death of Vera Martel seem to be the result of an automobile accident."

"Then it is your contention that both Carter Gilman and Glamis Barlow are responsible for the death of Vera Martel? That Glamis Barlow at least became his accessory after the fact?"

"That is a correct statement of my position," Hamilton Burger snapped.

"Now, Your Honor," Perry Mason said, "the vice of this sort of an examination becomes apparent. The prosecution *is* trying to use this Court as a means by which he can entrap the person whom he intends to name as a codefendant in the case just as soon as this hearing has been concluded. We insist that it is incompetent, irrelevant and immaterial whether or not Glamis Barlow was in that building at those times, unless the district attorney can positively show *first* that Vera Martel was there at that time, that the defendant was there at that time and that the murder took place at that time and place."

"We intend to show it by inference," Hamilton Burger said.

"Until the proper foundation can be laid, the question of the movements of Glamis Barlow becomes incompetent, irrelevant and immaterial," Perry Mason said, "at least as far as the present question is concerned. It can now only be construed as an attempt to impeach the veracity of Glamis Barlow who was the prosecution's own witness. They can't impeach their own witnesses. They are bound by her testimony. That is the penalty the prosecution must pay for calling a potential defendant to the stand and forcing her to answer questions before she can have the benefit of counsel."

Judge Alvord said, "I am inclined to agree with the defense, Mr. Burger. At this time, at any rate, the movements of Glamis Barlow would seem to have no possible bearing on the guilt or innocence of this defendant, unless you first show the presence of Vera Martel in that room at that time."

Hamilton Burger flushed. "I feel that the Court is penalizing me because I disagreed with Your Honor in regard to the expediency of calling Glamis Barlow as a witness."

"You may feel any way you want," Judge Alvord said. "I am trying to protect the substantial interests of justice. I advised you some time ago that you had apparently made out a prima-facie case against this defendant as far as a preliminary hearing is concerned. You insisted on going ahead in order to lay a foundation for what now appears to be an attempt to entrap a codefendant in a situation where she would make a statement under oath before she had been advised that she was going to be a codefendant in the case."

Hamilton Burger said, "Very well. I am forced to accept the ruling of the Court, but before I do so I am going to lay a broader foundation. Mrs. Kirk, were you alone in your breakfast nook at the time you mention?"

"No, sir. My daughter, Madeline, was with me."

"How old is Madeline?"

"She is nineteen."

"That is about Glamis Barlow's age?"

"A year younger."

"Do you know of your own knowledge whether your daughter Madeline and Glamis Barlow are friendly?"

"They are quite friendly in a casual sort of way; that is, as neighbors. They don't have double dates together and they move in different social circles, but they are quite friendly as neighbors."

"Do you know of your own knowledge how long this friendship has been going on?"

"For approximately two years."

"And Madeline was with you in the breakfast nook at the time you mention?"

"Yes."

"How were you seated?"

"We were seated at a table and looking out the window."

"Were you both on the same side of the table?"

"Yes. That is, it's not exactly a table. It's a sort of counter—I might say, a combination bar and table—a food bar—on which food can be served. It looks out to the north and over the backyard."

"Was your daughter facing the same direction that you were?"

"Yes, sir. She was seated beside me."

"Did you comment to your daughter on anything unusual that you saw at that time?"

Judge Alvord glanced at Mason. "Any objection on the part of the defense?"

"No objection," Mason said.

Judge Alvord said, "Well, it seems to me counsel is entitled to lay the foundation for his testimony but this is certainly going far afield. The defendant isn't bound by any conversation which may have taken place between this witness and her daughter."

"There is no objection by the defense," Mason said. "As a matter of fact, we welcome the situation, because once the prosecution has opened the door by showing a part of this conversation we are entitled to show it all on cross-examination."

Judge Alvord smiled slightly and said, "Under those circumstances, the witness may answer the question."

"Just a minute, just a minute," Hamilton Burger said hastily. "I . . . on second thought, Your Honor, I will withdraw the question."

"Very well," Judge Alvord said.

"I am now going to renew my request," Hamilton Burger said. "I ask this witness to relate to the Court what it was she saw that was unusual on the morning of the thirteenth while she was in the breakfast nook, facing toward the workroom of the defendant in this case."

"Same objection," Mason said.

"Same ruling," Judge Alvord said. "At this time the objection is sustained."

Hamilton Burger made no attempt to conceal his exasperation. He said, "May I have a moment, Your Honor?" and walked over to engage in a whispered consultation with Edwardo Deering.

Deering seemed to have a very positive idea in regard to an approach and after a few moments Hamilton Burger nodded.

"Very well," he said, "I will temporarily withdraw this witness from the stand, with the idea, if the Court please, that I am going to lay a proper foundation so that the question I want her to answer will be relevant."

"Very well," Judge Alvord said. "I may once more point out, Mr. Prosecutor, that you have established a prima-facie case, that the deeper you go into this case the more avenues you open up, the more possibility there is that complications may develop."

"I think I know what I'm doing, if the Court please," Hamilton Burger said.

"I hope you do," Judge Alvord commented drily. "The Court wishes to state, however, that Carter Gilman is the defendant in *this* case. But quite apparently your more recent witnesses have been called for the purpose of involving Glamis Barlow, who is *not* a defendant. The Court feels that if witnesses are to be called with the idea of involving Glamis Barlow, she should be a defendant and, as such, should have counsel who could subject the witnesses to searching cross-examination."

"I think I understand the Court's position," Hamilton Burger said, "and I'm quite certain I understand what I have in mind.

"I now wish to call Glenn Beaumont McCoy."

The door of the witness room opened and McCoy, a tall, slightly stooped individual in the early fifties, walked with loose-jointed deliberation to the stand, raised his hand, took the oath, and then seated himself on the witness chair.

"Where do you reside, Mr. McCoy?" Deering asked, while Hamilton Burger, seated at the table, was busily engaged in scribbling notes on a pad of legal foolscap.

"Nevada."

"Where were you residing on the thirteenth of this month?"

"Las Vegas, Nevada."

"What is your occupation?"

"I am a card dealer."

"Are you acquainted with Glamis Barlow?"

"I know her by sight."

"How many times have you seen her?"

"I can't recall offhand. Several times."

"Where have you seen her?"

"At the place where I am employed."

"Did you see her on the evening of the thirteenth of this month?"

"I did."

"Where?"

"Now, just a moment, if the Court please," Mason said. "I wish to interpose an objection on the ground that all of this is incompetent, irrelevant and immaterial."

"I propose to connect it up," Deering said.

"That isn't sufficient," Mason said. "An attempt is now being made to try Glamis Barlow as a codefendant with Carter Gilman. While I am representing Carter Gilman as his attorney I am not representing Glamis Barlow and I am not prepared to cross-examine witnesses who may testify to things that would involve Glamis Barlow in the commission of this crime. I think she is entitled to her own counsel."

"I think so, too," Judge Alvord said.

"Just a minute," Hamilton Burger announced, getting to his feet. "Before the Court rules on this objection I should like to state that it is the contention of the prosecution that Carter Gilman killed Vera Martel, that he took wax impressions of the keys in her key container, that he had keys made from those impressions, that he delivered those keys to Glamis Barlow and that she, in accordance with a common purpose, went to Las Vegas, Nevada, on the evening of the thirteenth and, using the keys given her by the defendant, entered the Las Vegas office of Vera Martel for the purpose of searching through papers in order to find some incriminating document."

"Incriminating to whom?" Judge Alvord said.

"Incriminating to both Glamis Barlow and Carter Gilman," Burger said.

"If the Court please," Mason said, "I think that is the wildest conjecture on the part of the district attorney. If Glamis Barlow entered that office for the purpose of getting a document which incriminated her in some way that is an entirely different case."

"Not if she got the key which opened the office from Carter Gilman," Hamilton Burger said. "And, furthermore, in order to show a joint purpose and a collaboration, we propose to show that fingerprints of the defendant, Carter Gilman, were found in the Las Vegas office of Vera Martel, and that this office as well as the Los Angeles office had literally been wrecked by someone who had pulled papers from the files and strewn them over the floor in a frantic search for some documents."

Judge Alvord was visibly impressed by Burger's statement.

"Can the prosecutor show *when* those fingerprints were made?" Mason asked. "Can he show those fingerprints were not made at a time prior to the death of Vera Martel?"

"The time is immaterial," Burger snapped.

Judge Alvord pursed his lips, then slowly nodded. "In a public office, Mr. Prosecutor, an office where the public is invited by implication, fingerprints are not necessarily incriminating evidence unless it can be shown those prints were made at a time when the public was supposed to be excluded or because of a direct connection with some crime."

"Not when the man who made those prints is shown to have transported the body of his victim in his automobile," Hamilton Burger protested.

Judge Alvord frowned. "This is a very close question, gentlemen," he said. "I have been somewhat impatient with the district attorney's methods here, but in view of this latest statement and the possible testimony of this witness I am beginning to see an overall pattern which may be well within the permissible strategy of counsel for the People."

"I still insist that it's incompetent, irrelevant and immaterial," Mason said, "until the district attorney first proves that the keys came from this defendant and that the document which Glamis Barlow was seeking was jointly incriminating."

"I am inclined to think, in view of the manner in which the evidence is now developing," Judge Alvord said, "that this may be permissible as tending to prove motivation. However, I will state to the prosecution, as I have stated several times before, that the prosecution has already made out a prima-facie case. If it intends to go ahead and try to prove a lot of details, such as motivation, it is going to open the door to a showing by the defense on those same matters.

"I would also like to point out that if these matters which would properly be a part of the case in the Superior Court are brought into the case at this time, and if it should then appear that the defendant is able to undermine the theory of the prosecution on any one of these matters, that weakens the case of the prosecution.

"Attempting to prove too much and failing in part of it may be just as fatal as attempting to prove too little."

"I think I know what I am doing," Hamilton Burger said. "I want to get this matter before the Court. I want to get these witnesses on the stand. I want to get their testimony in his case. I am willing to take my chances in the event any one of these factors in the case are discredited."

"Very well," Judge Alvord said. "I think, however, I would like to have a statement from you first as to what you expect to prove by this witness."

"We expect to prove that this witness is acquainted with Glamis Barlow, that he has seen her several times in Las

Vegas, that he has positively identified Glamis Barlow as the young woman he saw surreptitiously leaving the office of Vera Martel.

"The office of Vera Martel in Las Vegas is not in an office building but is on the second floor of a building which has a gambling establishment on the lower floor. Some of the upstairs rooms are devoted to apartments and there are a few offices. It happens that the office of Vera Martel is directly opposite the apartment occupied by this witness, an apartment which is given to him as part of his compensation as a card dealer in the casino downstairs.

"We expect to show that this witness saw Glamis Barlow surreptitiously leave the office of Vera Martel. We expect to show that the next morning the office of Vera Martel was found to have been burglarized and that files had been looted, papers strewn over the floor and that there was every evidence of a hasty search for some document, a search which presumably was successful."

"May I ask the precise time that this took place?" Mason asked.

"The time was precisely nine fifteen in the evening," Hamilton Burger said. "The witness can fix the time by reason of a radio program that had just given the time. And, if the Court please, we also expect to show the fingerprints of the defendant, Carter Gilman, were found in that office."

"We renew our objection," Mason said. "This is all by way of inference. Let the prosecution first prove that the defendant in this case turned over a key to Glamis Barlow."

"I think we can sufficiently establish that fact by inference at this stage of the case," Hamilton Burger said.

"Moreover," Mason said, "a witness can't testify as to a person's manner in leaving a room as to that manner being surreptitious. That is sheer conclusion."

"Not in this case," Hamilton Burger snapped. "There are a dozen things that show a consciousness of guilt: the tiptoe exit, the look up and down the corridor, the glance back over the shoulder, the quiet closing of the door."

"Then let him testify to those dozen things," Mason said, "and I'll cross-examine him on each one. But he can't give his conclusion."

Judge Alvord thought for a few moments, then reached a sudden decision. "The Court is going to take this matter under advisement," he said. "I'm going to look up some authorities this afternoon and this evening, and tomorrow morning at ten o'clock I'll make a ruling.

"Does the defense have any objection to a continuation of the case until ten o'clock tomorrow morning?"

"We have none," Mason said.

"Very well," Judge Alvord said, "the case is continued until ten o'clock tomorrow morning. The Court will take its ruling under advisement and announce its decision on this point at ten o'clock tomorrow morning. In the meantime, the defendant is remanded to the custody of the sheriff. Court is adjourned until ten A.M. tomorrow. All witnesses under subpoena will return at that time."

CHAPTER THIRTEEN

As soon as court had adjourned, Mason, his eyes tense with concentration, said to Paul Drake, "All right, Paul, I want some action and I want it fast. Who's the best polygraph operator in this area? I want to give some of my people a lie-detector test. Let's find out who's lying."

"For my money, Cartman Jasper is about the best—but who's going to take a lie-detector test? Carter Gilman is in custody and you can't give him a lie-detector test without the consent of the police and the prosecutors. Glamis Barlow is being held as a material witness and . . ."

"Primarily I'm thinking of Nancy Gilman," Mason said. "There's a woman who is something of an enigma. She has too much poise, too much polish, too much sex, in a nice sort of a way. She's dynamite and you're never going to be able to tell what she's thinking unless you can break below the surface."

"All right, what do you want me to do?"

"Get Cartman Jasper in one of your offices. Get him to set up his equipment all ready for a lie-detector test."

"And you're going to run Nancy Gilman?"

"That's right," Mason said.

He turned to Della Street. "Della, will you get Nancy Gilman and tell her that I want her in my office, that I want to talk with her?"

Della Street nodded.

"Stay with her," Mason said. "Take her right up to the office and wait for me."

As Della left, Mason turned to Paul Drake and said, "You get on the telephone and get Cartman Jasper up there and I may want to give you a lie-detector test, too."

"Me?" Drake exclaimed in surprise.

"Exactly," Mason said. "You might become a key witness in this case."

"How come?"

"This man McCoy may be the key to the whole thing. He'll swear that he saw Glamis Barlow leaving the office of Vera Martel at nine fifteen. Now, your notes show that Glamis Barlow was playing the slot machines in a casino up to nine eleven. She wouldn't have had time to get to Vera's place, have gone in, ransacked it and left by nine fifteen."

"Remember," Drake said, "that after she broke away and dashed out into a taxi, I don't know where she went."

"But," Mason said, "you called me and I sent you out to see Steve Barlow and you found her there."

"That, of course, was some time later."

"How much later?"

"Well, that was . . . well, she'd been gone three quarters of an hour."

"But up to nine eleven she was playing the slot machines?"

"Up to nine eleven she was playing the slot machines."

"Any chance you could be wrong on the time?"

"None whatever. Not unless I misread my wristwatch."

"Well, you're a hell of a detective if you can't tell the time from your wristwatch," Mason said. "Don't start introducing a negative element when you get on the witness stand. You were watching her at nine fifteen?"

"I was watching her play slot machines from forty minutes past eight until nine eleven," Drake said, "and then I didn't lose sight of the cab she was in until nine twelve."

"That's better," Mason said. "Get positive about it. Now then, you go get on the phone and get Cartman Jasper all set up in your office. I'm going to keep Della Street and Nancy Gilman waiting until I know that you're all ready to give a lie-detector test. Then I'm going to go to my office, try to cross-examine Nancy into telling me the truth, and then we're going to spring a lie detector on her."

"What's the truth?" Drake asked.

"The truth," Mason said, "is that she must have known Vera Martel."

"And Vera Martel was blackmailing her over something in her past?" Drake asked.

"It must have been some sort of a new angle on blackmail," Mason said. "Burger is maneuvering for position, trying to get us out on a limb. However, as Judge Alvord has pointed out, they've made a prima-facie case against Carter Gilman long ago and he is going to get bound over for murder unless we can dope this thing out within the next few hours, find out exactly what did happen and prove that he's innocent."

"You can never prove he's innocent in the face of this evidence," Drake said. "Hell's bells, the minute he went up to that locksmith with the impression of keys to Vera Martel's apartment and offices he was licked. The evidence of the sawdust is bad enough, but that key business has him so far behind the eight ball even you can't get him out."

"I know," Mason said, "but there's one person who can get him out."

"Who?"

"Hamilton Burger."

"Are you crazy?" Drake asked.

Mason shook his head. "Hamilton Burger is so eager to get a case built up where he'll have two of my clients so firmly enmeshed in a fabric of falsehood that they can never get clear, that he's losing sight of the fact Judge Alvord is going to upset his apple cart if he falls down on any element of the case."

"What element is he going to fall down on?"

"Glamis Barlow breaking into Vera Martel's office."

"Oh, look, Perry," Drake said. "That's simply a question of a mistake in the time element. Either McCoy or I was mistaken on the time."

"You don't sound too damn positive," Mason said.

"I'm positive, all right," Drake said, "but it's easy to make a mistake in the time. You put too much stress on this time element and McCoy will weaken on the witness stand and say, 'Well, I thought it was nine fifteen but I might have heard wrong. I guess it could have been ten fifteen.' "

Mason said, "*You* be certain that *you* don't weaken on the time element because I think we're on the trail of something."

"On the trail of what?"

"I wish I knew," Mason said. "Get busy and get Cartman Jasper up there in your office. If you can't get him, get someone else that's good, but have someone there just as fast as he can get in and get a polygraph set up."

"They like to do that polygraph work in their own offices," Drake said. "They're all equipped for it and—"

"I know, I know," Mason interrupted impatiently. "It isn't what *they* like in this case, it's what *I* like. They have portable lie detectors that they can bring in and set up, and if Nancy is a good reactor we can find out a lot within fifteen minutes after we start running her on the macine."

"Okay," Drake said, "I'll get Jasper."

Mason looked at his watch. "I'm going to give Della Street about a fifteen-minute head start," he said. "I think she can hold Nancy there that long and by that time Nancy is going to be just a little apprehensive."

"And then you come in?" Drake asked.

"Then I come in," Mason said.

"Okay," Drake told him. "I'll get hold of Jasper. I'm quite certain I can reach him. We'll be ready whenever you come in."

CHAPTER FOURTEEN

MASON LATCHKEYED the door of his private office to find Nancy Gilman plainly impatient and Della Street desperately trying to hold her.

As Mason opened the door Nancy Gilman was on her feet and apparently headed for the exit door.

Della Street, however, between her and the exit door, was saying, "I'm sure he'll be here any minute and it's quite important, Mrs. Gilman. He—"

Mason said, "Hello, everybody. Sit down, Mrs. Gilman. I have a few questions."

Nancy Gilman gave him the benefit of her super-magnetic smile, then suddenly her mouth was firm. "I have a few questions myself, Mr. Mason," she said.

"What are they?" Mason asked, making a surreptitious motion with his wristwatch to Della, indicating that he was stalling for time.

"I am *not* going to have Glamis shut up in jail like a common felon simply because they want her as a witness," she said. "Isn't there some procedure by which she can put up bail and be released?"

"Quite definitely," Mason said cheerfully.

"Well, why don't we do that?"

"Because at the present time I don't want to get in the position of representing both her and your husband."

"Then we'll get some other attorney to represent her," Mrs. Gilman said decisively.

"Exactly," Mason said. "That's one of the things I want to talk to you about. I want you to get a lawyer for her."

"I think this case has been a farce as far as justice is concerned," Nancy said. "Here is Hartley Elliott, a man of the highest moral character, a young man whose only fault was being loyal to his friends, thrown into jail for contempt of court. Here is Glamis, a young woman of refinement and delicacy thrown into a cell with hardened prostitutes and exposed to all sorts of indignities simply because the district attorney wants to have her as a witness."

"Listen," Mason said, "let *me* tell *you* something about the facts of life, Mrs. Gilman. You can get an attorney who can get Glamis Barlow released on bail without the slightest difficulty. You don't even need to call it bail. You put up a bond for her appearance as a witness and the court lets her out."

"Well, why don't we do it?" Nancy asked. "Why haven't *you* made arrangements to do it, Mr. Mason? Even if you couldn't represent both Glamis and Carter you could at least have arranged for some other attorney."

"Because," Mason said, "the minute she puts up a bond and steps out of custody as a material witness she'll be arrested as a codefendant. She'll then be charged with being an accessory after the fact in the murder or she'll be charged as a codefendant in the murder. Then Hamilton Burger will file a joint information against Glamis and your husband and try them both for the murder of Vera Martel.

"And once she's arrested for murder she can't get out on bail. Once she's arrested for murder, Hamilton Burger simply has to go through with the case, to save his face if for no other reason. Once she's arrested for murder she has no sympathy from either the court or the public. But so long as a good-looking girl like Glamis is being held as a material witness at the whim of the district attorney, she has the sympathy of both the court and the public.

"For your information, this way of handling the case is making the judge angry at the prosecutor.

"Now then, does that answer your question?"

Nancy Gilman thought that over for a few moments, then when she spoke there was a decided change in her manner.

"I still think it's the most absurd thing I ever heard of in my life," Nancy said. "Carter wouldn't hurt a fly and Glamis has no more idea of what happened than . . . well, she's completely innocent."

"What about those people who were going to testify that they saw her running out of the workshop?"

"Bosh and nonsense!"

"Do *you* know where Glamis was that morning?"

"I don't know, no. I was asleep. But I know what Muriell told me, and Muriell said there was absolutely no possibility that Glamis could have got back in the house, got her clothes off and come out to stand in the hall by the time Muriell came down from the attic. It's absurd!"

"The matter seems to hinge," Mason said, "on whether you knew Vera Martel in her lifetime."

"I never heard of the creature."

"You wouldn't have paid her any blackmail?"

"I wouldn't have paid anyone any blackmail, Mr. Mason. If anybody tried to blackmail me I'd kick them down the front steps.

"Look at me, Mr. Mason. Believe me and believe my sincerity. I've lived my own life. I haven't conformed to the conventions. I've had an illegitimate child. You know that. I could have married the father of Glamis Barlow in order to give the child a name. When he learned I was in trouble and started trying to save his own skin I lost all respect for him. I made up my mind that I'd have my own child in my own way. I came out here and disappeared and defied all of his efforts to find me then or later.

"Anybody could dig into my past and find a lot of things that showed I'd been untrue to the conventions, but I defy anybody to show that I've ever been untrue to myself or to my own best convictions. And as long as I feel that way I'll throw any blackmailer out of the house."

Mason said, "If we could establish those facts it might help a lot."

"What do you mean, if we could establish them?"

Mason said, "Mrs. Gilman, I want you to look me in the eyes. Are you lying?"

She looked him in the eyes and said, "No, I'm not lying. I don't stoop to falsehoods. I can afford to be myself and I don't like deceit, I don't like falsehoods, I don't like hypocrisy."

"All right," Mason said, "here's my idea. I want you to take a lie-detector test today, right now. I am going to let the newspapers know about the results of that lie-detector test. I want to establish that you did not know Vera Martel and that she was not blackmailing you."

For a moment Nancy Gilman's eyes seemed to waver.

"If," Mason said, "you are telling the truth, if you have a scorn of hypocrisy and of falsehood, you have absolutely nothing to fear. You can pass the lie-detector test with flying colors."

"But," she said, "suppose I'm nervous? Suppose the man who gives the lie-detector test doesn't appreciate the difference between nervousness and the reaction of one who is telling an untruth?"

"The man I have in mind," Mason said, "is thoroughly competent. He's not going to be fooled by anything of that sort. He'll talk with you until he gets your normal level, your normal reactions, and then he'll ask you questions. If you're lying, don't take the test. Just leave the office quietly and I'll try to do the best I can for your husband. And if you're lying I'm afraid there's not much I can do."

"I'm not lying."

"Then if you could prove that you're not lying," Mason said, "it might help your husband—and your daughter."

"Where do I take this lie-detector test?" she asked.

Mason nodded to Della Street. "Take her down to Paul Drake's office, Della. Cartman Jasper is there, Mrs. Gilman. You'll take the lie-detector test in a room where you won't be disturbed, where there are no distractions, where your reactions will be measured by a very delicate machine which registers your blood pressure, your respiration, your electrical skin-resistance."

"What do all those things have to do with it?"

"If," Mason said, "you're a good reactor you can't tell a falsehood without having a change in blood pressure, probably distinctive changes in the rate and type of respiration and changes in the electrical resistance of your skin.

If, as you say, you have scorned falsehoods, if you have never had experience in lying, you'll make a perfect subject and Jasper will be able to give you a clean bill of health.

"If I can tell the newspaper reporters that you took a lie-detector test, if they can interview Cartman Jasper and find that you never knew Vera Martel, had no reason to fear her and weren't planning to pay her any blackmail, it will be a tremendous moral advantage. Of course, we can't use the results of a lie-detector test in court, but the resulting public sentiment which naturally will come from such a test will greatly enhance the difficulties of a district attorney."

Nancy Gilman turned to Della Street. Her manner was that of royalty. "Please take me to where I am to go, Miss Street," she said. "I am ready."

Della Street said, "This way, please," and left the office.

Five minutes later Della Street was back.

"Everything all set?" Mason asked.

"Everything's all set," she said. "Paul Drake has her and Cartman Jasper in his interrogation room. There's one of those trick mirrors and we can look through and see what's going on without being seen. The room is bugged so we can hear what's being said and there's even a mirror in the ceiling so that you can watch the results of the needles on the polygraph machine as she answers questions."

Mason grinned. "Let's go."

"Do you know just what you hope to accomplish?" Della Street asked.

Mason shook his head. "I'm fighting for time and I'm

fighting a tough combination of seemingly insurmountable difficulties and overwhelming evidence. When a lawyer gets in that position the only thing for him to do is to take the initiative and keep moving. Let's go."

They walked down the corridor to Drake's office. The receptionist nodded and, putting her finger to her lips for silence, tiptoed down the corridor and opened a door.

Paul Drake was standing in a darkened room looking through a one-way mirror into a questioning room where Nancy Gilman was seated in front of a polygraph machine. A pressure cuff was around her arm, electrodes on her hand and a coil placed around her chest so as to register the rhythm of her breathing.

Paul Drake said in a hoarse whisper, "He's made quite an impression on her already. He got her to select a number between one and ten and then not only told her what the number was but showed her her graph in order to show how her blood pressure indicated the number when he came to it. I think he now has her in the right frame of mind to go ahead with the test."

Cartman Jasper adjusted the needles on the machine. They could hear his voice through the microphone-speaking device which relayed sounds from the other office.

"Now, Mrs. Gilman, I am going to ask you to answer all of the questions I ask, either yes or no. If it is necessary to make any explanation or to elaborate on your answer, wait until the test is completed. But just answer these questions as I ask them, yes or no. Do you understand?"

Nancy Gilman nodded.

"Please don't move in any way during the brief period in which I am giving you this test. Sit perfectly relaxed and avoid any muscular movement. Try to think only about the questions and the answers to the questions. Are you ready?"

"Yes."

"You are seated comfortably?"

"Yes."

Jasper, in a toneless voice, said, "Is your first name Nancy?"

"Yes."

There was an interval of some ten seconds, then Jasper gave the second question. "Are you the mother of a daughter named Glamis?"

"Yes."

"Do you smoke?"

"Yes."

"Are you married to Carter Gilman?"

"Yes."

"Did you ever know a person named Vera M. Martel?"

"No."

"Did you have breakfast this morning?"

"Yes."

"Has anyone tried to blackmail you during the past three months?"

"No."

"Of your own knowledge, do you know who killed Vera M. Martel?"

"No."

"Are you interested in photography?"

"Yes."

"Do you know a person named Steven A. Barlow?"

"Yes."

"Would you object if I should ask you an embarrassing

personal question while the polygraph tested the truth of your answer?"

There was a moment of silence, then she said, "Yes."

Cartman Jasper said, "Very well, Mrs. Gilman, we'll rest for a few moments and then I am going to repeat the same questions again in exactly the same order."

Mason, who had been looking at the mirror which showed the graph made by the three needles on the chart, said in a puzzled voice, "She's telling the truth."

"Unless she doesn't react," Della Street said.

"Of course she reacts," Mason said. "Look at the reaction that took place when Jasper asked her that last test question. She's a good reactor but . . ."

"What is it?" Della Street asked.

"When they asked her about her daughter, Glamis," Mason said, "there was a distinct reaction. Of course, it may be just a matter of adjustment or something that caused an isolated reaction. However, you've got it in her pulse, her blood pressure, her respiration and her skin resistance. She's a very good reactor and something happened there. . . . Let's see what happens again."

Once more Jasper went through the questions. Once more there was a very definite reaction when he questioned her about Glamis.

Mason turned to Della Street, said, "He'll run her through once more. We'd probably better go back to the office. She may want to come and see us when she's finished, and it wouldn't be advisable to have her know we were watching."

Paul Drake followed them to the door. "Do you want to try to break her down, Perry? I think you're wasting time. I think she's telling the truth."

"There's something about Glamis that bothers her," Mason said thoughtfully.

"Why shouldn't there be? Glamis is an illegitimate child and I suppose that beneath Nancy Gilman's somewhat casual exterior she keenly appreciates the position her indiscretion has put Glamis in."

Mason nodded. "That *probably* accounts for it," he said, "but there certainly was a very definite reaction there. We'll see what Cartman Jasper says. Tell him to come down to my office after he's finished, and unless Nancy Gilman wants to see me about something, let her go home. She was, I believe, in something of a hurry."

Mason and Della Street went back to their office. Twenty minutes later Cartman Jasper came in with the graphs of the examination folded in his hand.

"What do you think?" Mason asked.

Jasper said, "She's telling the truth all the way through, Mason, as far as the case is concerned. She never knew Vera Martel, she hasn't been blackmailed, but she's lying about Glamis Barlow."

"You mean Glamis Barlow isn't her daughter?" Mason asked.

"I don't know," Jasper said. "I'd have to make up a set of test questions about Glamis and ask her those in order to find out the truth. But there's something in connection with Glamis that causes her to have an emotional reaction."

"You knew that Glamis was illegitimate?" Mason asked.

"Paul Drake told me that, but I don't think that accounts for it, Mason. I think there's something else. There's some emotional disturbance there in connection with the statement that she had a daughter named Glamis Barlow."

Mason frowned thoughtfully. "Now, suppose Glamis isn't her daughter," he said.

"That could very well be," Jasper admitted.

"Gosh, what an opportunity for a blackmailer *that* would be!" Mason said.

CHAPTER FIFTEEN

MASON, pacing his office, said to Paul Drake, "Hang it, Paul, there's something wrong with this whole case. Somebody drew ten thousand dollars out of a bank and got an even amount—ten thousand dollars. It was to be used to pay blackmail. Don't tell me anyone could do that without leaving a trace."

"They did it," Drake said, "and they didn't leave a trace. I've exhausted every lead I can think of."

Mason said, "I'm sitting on top of a volcano with ten thousand dollars in my safe. That ten thousand dollars is probably evidence. I'm going to have to do something about it. I don't want to betray a client, but I can't conceal evidence. I'm going to have to get in touch with the police and tell them that I found this money. If the police should find out I have the money before I reported it I would be in quite a fix. Every hour that I have that money, every minute that I have it without reporting it, I'm skating on thin ice."

"Well, why don't you report it, then?"

Mason shook his head. "I'm not going to sell a client down the river, Paul. I'm going to find out where that money came from before I make a move. Now, you've followed instructions and had your men working on Vera Martel's activities for the week preceding her death?"

Drake nodded, said, "I'm spending a lot of money having men try to uncover every bit of information they can about her. No one knows much. She was working on several cases. She was away from her office for two days, but that was nearly ten days before she was murdered."

"Where did she go?" Mason asked.

"Search me," Drake said. "We haven't been able to find out."

"Find out," Mason said. "There was an air travel card and a couple of gasoline credit cards in her purse. Get busy. Find out where the gasoline credit card was used. Start right now and see what you can find out about that air travel card."

"That was ten days before the thirteenth," Drake protested.

"I don't give a damn when it was," Mason said. "There's something missing in this case and I want to find it before the police do. You can imagine the spot I'll be in if the police find out about—"

The telephone rang.

Della Street picked it up, said, "Hello," then said, "Muriell on the phone, Mr. Mason. She's been crying, is pretty much upset."

Mason nodded, said, "Listen in, Della," and picked up the receiver.

Muriell's voice came over the wire. She was so emotionally upset that it was hard to understand her.

"Mr. Mason," she said, choking back sobs, "I've—I've been disloyal. . . . I've—I've sold you down the river."

"Go on," Mason said. "Try and be as brief as possible, Muriell. There may not be much time. What did you do?"

"The police gave me—I guess it was a third degree. They got me in the district attorney's office and they really dragged me over the coals and they threatened me and . . . well, I told them about everything."

"The money?" Mason asked.

"The money," she said.

"What did you tell them about it?"

"Everything."

"What else?"

"I told them everything I knew."

"About your father disappearing?"

"Yes."

"About the fact that you telephoned me?"

"Everything, Mr. Mason. . . . Oh, I don't know what made me do it! It just seemed as though pressures were building up inside of me and they kept hammering away: hammering, hammering, hammering all the time."

"When did this happen?" Mason asked.

"Right after court adjourned. I was picked up and hurried into this district attorney's office."

"Why didn't you refuse to go?"

"I didn't have an opportunity. A policewoman just took me on one side and an officer on the other and they said, 'Right this way. The D. A. wants to talk with you,' and there I was and . . . well, then they just seemed to know how to go about it, and I told them everything."

"Are you in any sort of custody?" Mason asked.

"No. They let me go but they served me with a subpoena. I'm going to have to be a witness tomorrow, Mr. Mason. *I'm going to have to be a witness against Daddy!* Oh, Mr. Mason, I just feel terrible. I don't know what to do."

"All right," Mason said, "you've gone this far. Now, don't get despondent, don't get the idea of jumping off a bridge or taking an overdose of sleeping pills. You've been served with a subpoena. You're going to have to be a witness. You can take it and I can take it. Now, quit worrying about it. Take a couple of aspirins and settle back and relax."

"But I've let you down terribly."

Mason said, "It's all right. I'll handle things."

Mason hung up the telephone, said to Paul Drake, "Well, that does it. I suppose that any minute now I'll be served with—"

He broke off as Lt. Tragg, accompanied by a plainclothes man, pushed open the door from the outer office.

"Well, hello, folks," Tragg said. "Caught you in conference, eh?"

Mason said, "It would help a lot if you'd have yourself announced, Tragg."

Tragg smiled and shook his head. "I've told you a dozen times, Mason, the taxpayers don't like it."

"And what's the urgent business that brings you here?" Mason asked.

Tragg smiled. "Well, now, Perry," he said, "the district attorney wants you as a witness."

"Me as a witness?" Mason asked.

"That's right," Tragg said. "A *subpoena duces tecum,* Mr. Mason, ordering that you be in court tomorrow morning at ten o'clock and that you bring with you the sum of ten thousand dollars in currency or any other currency or any other article which you picked up in the workshop of Carter Gilman at 6231 Vauxman Avenue on or about the thirteenth day of this month, or at any other time thereafter.

"I've warned you, Perry, that you shouldn't mix into things the way you do. Now, if you'd just spoken up and told the police about finding ten thousand dollars out there on the floor it might have simplified things a lot. But, no, you chose to keep your own counsel and now I'm sorry, Mason, but you're going to be a witness for the prosecution and I'm a little afraid Hamilton Burger is going to take a very dim view of suppressing evidence."

Lt. Tragg turned to the plain-clothes man and made a little gesture. "This is Perry Mason," he said. "I identify him."

The plain-clothes officer stepped forward and said, "A *subpoena duces tecum,* Mr. Mason. Here's the original, here's your copy. Be in court tomorrow morning at ten o'clock. Have the articles mentioned in the subpoena with you."

"That'll be all," Lt. Tragg said. "Be a little careful when it comes to cross-examining yourself, Mason. Don't be rough on yourself because you're going to be one of Hamilton Burger's star witnesses. I can't begin to tell you how much Hamilton Burger is looking forward to this."

Mason took the subpoena. Lt. Tragg walked to the exit door of the private office, held it open for the plain-clothes man, started out, turned, and suddenly the smile left his face. "If I told you I was sorry, Perry," he said, "I'd be giving aid and comfort to the enemy and might get a couple of demerits—so I won't tell you I'm sorry—I *won't* tell you I'm sorry."

"Thanks, Lieutenant," Mason said.

"Not at all," Tragg said, and closed the door.

"Well," Drake said lugubriously, "you insist on skating on thin ice and now you're trapped— Where does that leave you? Are you suppressing evidence?"

"Not necessarily," Mason said. "How am I supposed to know it's evidence? Nobody told me. All I've got to do is to prove that the title to that money is in my client, Carter Gilman, and I have a perfect right to it. I had Gilman sign a bill of sale giving me all of his right, title and interest in and to the contents of his workshop as a part of my fee; the contents to include everything that was in the workshop on the thirteenth."

"Well," Drake said, "you're going to have to prove that he owned the money. He—"

The telephone rang.

Della Street picked it up, said, "Yes . . . Yes . . . It's for you, Paul."

Drake came over and took the instrument, said, "Hello . . . Yes . . . *What!* . . . Good heavens!"

Della Street, listening to the detective's voice, moved a chair up for him and Drake dropped into it as though his knees had buckled.

"You're sure?" Drake asked. "Now, wait a minute. There can't be any . . . Oh, good Lord . . . Well, that does it . . . All right. Now, look, there was an air travel card in Vera Martel's purse. There were also a couple of credit cards for gasoline. Find out where those cards were last used. Get busy. I want a report on that right now. . . . All right, I'll be here for a while. Call me back."

Drake said, "Perry, I hate to be the one that breaks it to you, but this is it."

"What is it, Paul?"

"That money!" Drake said. "My operatives, checking

around in Las Vegas trying to find everything that Vera Martel had been doing during the last ten days of her life, found that on the third of the month she went to the bank and drew ten thousand dollars in cash."

Mason stood motionless, his face granite hard.

"All right," he said at length, "they can't prove it's the same money."

"That's the hell of it; they can," Drake said. "The banker wondered why she wanted that money in hundred-dollar bills and thought perhaps it was the payment of ransom in a kidnaping. He didn't dare delay things long enough to tip her off but he told her he had to go back to the vault to get enough hundreds. He was only gone half a minute, but during that time he managed to take the numbers of six of the one-hundred-dollar bills that he gave her. He has those numbers."

"Do the police know about it?" Mason asked.

"Not yet, but they will. The minute the newspapers blazon forth the fact that Hamilton Burger has called you as his star witness for the prosecution and that ten thousand dollars in cash figures in the deal, the banker will read the newspapers, come forward with the numbers on the bills and you're sunk."

Mason started pacing the floor. After a few minutes, the phone rang again.

Della Street, answering it, again nodded to Paul.

"For you," Della Street said.

"Well, thank heavens," Drake said. "We've got all the bad news now, so this is bound to be something good."

He moved over to the instrument, said, "Hello . . . Yes . . . This is Paul . . . Okay, thanks."

He hung up and said, "I was wrong, Perry."

"What is it this time?" Mason asked.

"Hartley Elliott," Paul Drake said. "They really gave him the works, Perry. They didn't put him in any nice separate cell where he would be treated like a gentleman. They didn't give him an opportunity for any special treatment. They threw him in the tank with a bunch of drunks. By the time he wallowed around in a lot of filth, after a couple of drunks had vomited all over him, he'd had all the jail he wanted. He sent word to the district attorney that he wanted out, that he'd go on the stand and testify tomorrow."

Mason said, "They couldn't do that to a man in only on contempt."

"They did it," Paul said, "and it worked. The D. A. fished him out of the tank and he's in the D. A.'s office now making an affidavit."

Mason might not have heard the detective. He turned and resumed his pacing of the office floor.

Della Street watched him apprehensively, her eyes following him, sick with concern.

Drake, standing uncomfortably, finally said, "Well, I guess I'm not doing any good here. I'll get out before someone else brings in some bad news."

Mason gave no sign that he had heard, nor did he say anything as Drake said lamely, "Well, so long. I'll see you folks later," and left the office.

The lawyer continued pacing the floor, back and forth, back and forth, his head bowed slightly in thought, his eyes level-lidded with concentration.

Della Street, knowing the lawyer's moods, sat quietly, watching him with eyes that showed the depths of her concern and sympathy.

Twenty minutes later, Mason finished pacing the floor, moved over to sit down at the office desk. The tips of his fingers drummed silently on the blotter.

"Can you salvage anything out of the situation?" Della Street asked.

"I can go down fighting," Mason said.

"How serious is it not reporting the finding of the ten thousand dollars?"

"I don't know," Mason said. "There aren't any precedents for it. I assumed the money belonged to my client—either Gilman or his wife; that it had been intended as a blackmail payment and that they could give me title to it."

"And as a blackmail payment it wouldn't have been evidence?"

"It might have been," Mason said, "but no one told me anything that indicated it was. Nobody would admit it. No one would admit getting that much money out of the bank. The reason for that is now apparent. They didn't."

"Then where did the money come from?" Della Street asked. "Why would Vera Martel leave her money there?"

"That," Mason said, "is what I'm trying to figure out. This is a new angle. The blackmailer comes to pay money to the person who is being blackmailed. Now, figure that one out."

The telephone rang again. Della Street picked up the receiver, said, "Paul Drake," and Mason, picking up his own phone, said, "Yes, Paul, what is it this time?"

"I don't know," Drake said. "All I know is that we checked on the air travel card of Vera Martel. She took a plane to Redding, California on the fourth. She was gone two days."

"Got a correspondent in Redding you can trust?" Mason asked.

"I have a good man there. He's an ex-cop, private operator and—"

"All right, get him," Mason said. "In a town the size of Redding, Vera Martel would stand out like a sore thumb. She got off the plane. She didn't have a car. Either someone met her or she went to a hotel or a motel. Find out. Call me back. Tell your man he's got two hours. We want the information by that time. Della Street and I are going out to dinner. You stay on the job. Get your man up in Redding working and get him working fast."

Mason hung up the phone and looked thoughtfully at Della Street. "Now, why the devil would Vera Martel go to Redding on the fourth of the month and stay for two days?"

Della Street shook her head. "It's all part of a puzzle—are you sure the solution lies with Vera Martel?"

"I can't find a key to it anywhere else," Mason said. "There's no place else to turn and . . ."

"And?" Della Street asked, as the lawyer's voice trailed off into silence.

"And," Mason said, "we're desperate."

"Feel you can eat?" Della Street asked.

Mason's grin was slightly forced. "I don't know," he said, "but I think I can. It isn't eating, it's taking on fuel, because we're going to be in a dog fight tomorrow. I guess Hamilton Burger's enjoying his dinner enough tonight for both of us. Let's go."

The lawyer and his secretary closed the door of the private office. Della Street slipped her hand into his and squeezed it, by the pressure giving him wordless assurance of her loyalty and sympathy.

The lawyer patted her shoulder, said, "It's all right, Della, I've dished it out and I guess I can take it if I have to."

"It seems so terribly one-sided," Della Street complained.

"I know," Mason said. "Usually, when things turn against you they go all the way. Come on, let's eat."

They sought out the dim light of their favorite cocktail bar, had a cocktail, then moved into the restaurant and ordered dinner.

Mason ate slowly, methodically, and in silence. Della Street, after the second bite, found that she couldn't touch the food and pushed her plate away.

There was no conversation. Della Street toyed with a water glass while Mason completed the task of eating.

When Mason had finished, Della Street walked over to the phone booth, called Drake's office.

Paul Drake's voice, seeming somewhat puzzled, said, "I'm striking some sort of pay dirt, Della, but I don't know what it is. Can Perry come to the phone?"

"I'll get him," Della Street said.

She returned to Mason's table and said, "Paul Drake is waiting on the telephone. He's got something but he can't evaluate it."

Mason nodded, pushed back his chair, walked wordlessly to the telephone booth, closed the door, said, "Hello, Paul. What is it?"

"My man in Redding," Drake said. "He's a good man.

He called in about ten minutes ago with a complete report. I have him waiting at the telephone."

"All right. What's the report?" Mason asked.

"Vera Martel arrived on a Pacific Airlines plane. She was met by Maureen Monroe. Maureen was waiting for her at the airport in a classy car and Vera Martel stepped into the car and went out to the Monroe home."

"All right," Mason said. "What about Maureen Monroe? Who is she?"

"Apparently she's quite the upper crust in Redding. Her father owns a few thousand acres of timberland, a couple of sawmills. She's the town's most attractive dish."

"All right. What did Vera do?"

"She went out to the Monroe residence. She was out there for a couple of hours, then Maureen drove her back to the hotel. Vera Martel got a room and took the first southbound plane."

"Where to?"

"Back to Los Angeles."

"Then what? Did she call on anyone we know?"

"I haven't found out what she did there," Drake said, "but her air travel card shows she took a plane to Las Vegas the next day."

"Can your man find out anything about what happened up there?"

"No. Maureen Monroe is in San Francisco or Los Angeles. Her father is someplace in Oregon."

Mason thought for a moment, then said, "Give me the number of the telephone where this guy is waiting in Redding, Paul. What's his name?"

"Alan Hancock. I told him to wait at a telephone. I can call him and have him call you there at the booth. It may be easier than for you to try and put through a long-distance call."

"Okay," Mason said. "I'll wait here. Tell him to call me at the restaurant."

Mason returned to the table.

"What was it?" Della Street asked.

Mason told her.

"But, Chief," Della Street said, "that was . . . gosh, that was more than a week before the murder. More than that. It couldn't have had anything to do with the murder."

"How do we know?" Mason asked.

"Well . . . we don't," Della Street said.

"When you start putting a jigsaw puzzle together," Mason said, "you have to consider the sequence of events. The sequence may be equally as significant as the events themselves."

"I don't understand," Della Street said. "What sequence . . . ?"

A waiter approached the table and said, "There's a long-distance call for you, Mr. Mason, from Redding. A gentleman named Hancock says you're expecting the call. Do you wish to take it?"

Mason nodded. "Bring a telephone," he said. "I'll take it here at the table."

The waiter brought a phone, plugged in the jack and handed the instrument to Mason.

Mason said, "Hello, this is Perry Mason. . . . Yes, I'm expecting the call. Put him on."

A moment later, a man's voice said, "Mr. Mason, this is Mr. Drake's correspondent in Redding, Alan Hancock. He said you wanted to talk with me."

"That's right," Mason said. "What about this Monroe family? What can you tell me about them?"

"Mr. Monroe is the town's leading citizen."

"How old?" Mason asked.

"Oh, about fifty-two or fifty-three, I would judge. He's made a fortune in lumber."

"His wife?"

"She died a couple of years ago."

"Now, when Vera Martel came up to Redding," Mason said, "she had business with Mr. Monroe. Monroe sent his daughter down to pick Vera up— Now, do you have any inkling as to what the business could have been?"

"No, sir, I don't. I do know that Mr. Monroe must have been expecting this Martel woman. He made the drive down from Dunsmuir, went directly to his house, stayed there until after Miss Martel had departed and then had his daughter take Miss Martel to the hotel. Mr. Monroe left the next morning."

"What are his initials?" Mason asked.

"G. W.," Hancock said. "Stands for George Washington."

"What about the daughter? How old?"

"Right around twenty."

"Good-looking?"

"Beautiful."

"Ever been in any trouble?"

"Not that anyone knows about. She's a wonderful girl. She's engaged to be married."

"Oh-oh," Mason said. "When's the wedding?"

"Next month."

"What's the man's name?"

"Harvey C. Kimberly."

"What do you know about him?"

"Nothing. He's in New York, I believe. He's from Phoenix, Arizona. His family is very wealthy. There's quite a background of yachts and all that. But I guess the young fellow is all right. He's a bit older than she is—twenty-five, I believe."

Mason said, "All right. Dig up everything you can find in the line of newspaper publicity. There must have been quite a bit of it."

"Heavens yes, there was lots of publicity."

"Photographs of the fiancé and fiancée and the family?"

"That's right."

"You can put your hand on pictures of G. W. Monroe?"

"Oh, yes."

"How long will it take?"

"Not very long."

"When can you get a plane out of there?"

"Well, let's see. Tomorrow morning . . ."

"Forget it," Mason said. "Round up all of the pictures you can get. Get all of the newspaper stories. Find out everything you can, and then charter a plane about two or three o'clock in the morning that will get you down to Sacramento so you can pick up the first airliner from Sacramento in here. If you can't pick up a regular airliner, charter planes to get here. I want you to meet me here in court at ten o'clock in the morning. Drake will give you detailed instructions. Don't leave Redding until the last minute. Put in all the time you can scouting around up there and getting every bit of information and gossip you can pick up. I'll be seeing you at ten o'clock."

The lawyer hung up the telephone, turned to regard Della Street with thoughtful but unseeing eyes.

After a moment, she shifted her position and said, "Well?"

Suddenly Mason grinned. "Get Paul Drake on the phone," he said. "There's a rich young man, Harvey C. Kimberly, from Phoenix, Arizona; a background of wealth, yachts, polo ponies and what-not, but with it all he's supposed to be a good Joe who is probably trying to fit himself to carry on in the footsteps of an illustrious father and manage a family business which probably runs into the millions.

"Tell Paul I want everything we can get on Harvey C. Kimberly and I want it by ten o'clock tomorrow morning. I want—"

Suddenly Mason ceased speaking. His eyes again showed the extent of his concentration.

After a few moments, Della Street asked, "Anything else?"

Mason shook his head and said, "I'm toying with an idea, Della. It's the damnedest idea anyone ever had, but it accounts for the ten thousand dollars."

CHAPTER SIXTEEN

WORD HAD BEEN flashed around the courthouse and the courtroom was jammed as Judge Alvord took the bench.

"We'll resume the hearing of the Case of the People versus Gilman," he said.

"I may state to counsel that I am advised that the witness, Hartley Elliott, wishes to purge himself of contempt and is now willing to come forward.

"The Court will, therefore, direct that proceedings be interrupted for Mr. Elliott to again take the stand and he will then be given an opportunity to purge himself of the contempt."

Elliott emerged from the witness room.

Mason turned to Paul Drake. "Where the devil is Hancock?"

"The plane was late getting in," Drake said. "There's fog over the airport and they're having trouble with landings."

"Hang it!" Mason said. "He should have chartered a private plane and—"

"He'd have been in worse trouble on a private plane," Drake said. "The field is pretty well socked in. But they're bringing the planes in. Hancock was due in at eight thirty this morning. He probably has landed and is on his way to the courthouse now."

"Find out," Mason said. "Get someone to call the airport. See what's happened to his flight. I may have to ask for a continuance."

Hartley Elliott seated himself on the witness stand.

"Young man," Judge Alvord said, "I understand that you have decided to subject yourself to the orders of the Court in order to purge yourself of contempt."

"Yes, Your Honor."

"Very well," Judge Alvord said, "the district attorney will resume questioning this witness. If the witness answers all questions fairly and willingly the witness will be deemed to have purged himself of the contempt and the sentence will be revoked. Proceed, Mr. District Attorney."

Hamilton Burger, his face indicating triumphant pleasure, said, "Mr. Elliott, I am going to ask you when you first saw Glamis Barlow on the morning of the thirteenth. Understand now, I am asking you when you *first* saw her."

"I didn't leave her until after midnight," Elliott said.

"Very well. I will amend the question. After you had retired on the morning of the thirteenth, when was the next time you saw Glamis Barlow?"

"It was at eight twenty-five."

"You're certain of the time?"

"Yes, sir."

"And where were you at that time?"

"I was standing at the window of the bedroom I occupied in the Gilman house at 6231 Vauxman Avenue."

"And you saw Miss Barlow?"

"Yes."

"Where was she when you saw her?"

"She was emerging from the door of the workshop."

"Now, so there can be no misunderstanding as to what you mean by workshop, I am asking you to advance to the blackboard and point out the spot you mean on the diagram."

The witness did so.

Hamilton Burger said, "For the sake of the record, let it be shown that the witness has pointed to the rectangle marked 'Workshop' on the diagram, People's Exhibit B. That is correct, is it, Mr. Elliott?"

"Yes, sir."

"Now then, what did you see her do?"

Elliott hesitated perceptibly, then said, "She emerged from the door. She looked to right and left, then pulled the door shut, started walking, and then she ran around the house."

"Around the house? What do you mean?"

"She went in a southerly direction and I lost sight of her as she turned the corner."

"When did you next see her?" Hamilton Burger asked.

"About ten minutes later."

"And where did you see her?"

"I heard her voice in the corridor. I opened my bedroom door a crack and I saw her standing there garbed in an exceedingly revealing night garment. She was two thirds facing me and talking with Muriell. I felt that it would be embarrassing . . ."

"Never mind what you felt," Hamilton Burger said. "What did you see? What did you do?"

"I gently closed the door so that I would make no noise and so neither of the young women would know that I had seen them."

"Could you hear any of the conversation?"

"I heard Muriel say that she had been looking for her father and Glamis said sarcastically, 'In the attic,' or words to that effect."

"Cross-examine," Hamilton Burger said.

Then, before Mason could get to his feet, Hamilton Burger addressed the Court and said, "If the Court please, my next witness is going to be Mr. Perry Mason. Mr. Mason has been served with a *subpoena duces tecum* to bring certain articles of evidence into court that were surreptitiously and wrongfully removed from the premises at 6231 Vauxman Avenue.

"I am fully aware that it is unusual to subpoena a defense attorney, but the fact remains that where the defense attorney has certain knowledge of facts proving the commission of a crime the defense attorney is a proper witness. I feel, however, that so there can be no delay or misunderstanding, I am entitled to know at this time and before Mr. Mason cross-examines this witness whether he has brought into court the articles referred to in a *subpoena duces tecum* which was served upon him yesterday."

Judge Alvord's face showed some concern. "You are planning to call the defendant's attorney as a witness against the defendant himself?"

"Yes, Your Honor."

"Do you have anything to say, Mr. Mason?"

"Yes, Your Honor," Mason said. "I am entitled to have this case proceed in an orderly manner. I am entitled to cross-examine this witness. When the prosecutor puts me on the stand, if he chooses to do so, I will answer his questions at that time. I have never defied the process of this court or any other court, and there is no occasion for the district attorney to play to the galleries by making an announcement at this time, the effect of which primarily is to alert the press."

"That's not true," Hamilton Burger shouted. "I simply want to know whether I can proceed with my case without—"

"That will do, gentlemen, that will do," Judge Alvord interrupted. "The Court is inclined to feel that Mr. Mason is entitled at this time to cross-examine this witness. If the prosecutor had addressed the Court at the time the case was first called and asked more assurance as to whether counsel had obeyed a *subpoena duces tecum,* the Court might have considered the matter. But at this time the Court feels that the inquiry can well be suspended until after Mr. Mason's cross-examination of the witness, or perhaps until Mr. Mason himself has been called as a witness."

"Thank you, Your Honor," Mason said, and turned to look at Paul Drake.

Drake shook his head.

Mason approached the witness. "You have known Glamis Barlow for how long, Mr. Elliott?"

"Some two months."

"What is your occupation?"

"I am a manufacturer's agent."

"You represent several different manufacturers of merchandise?"

"Yes."

"Within what territory do you operate?"

"The State of California."

"You have the entire State of California for all of the manufacturers whom you represent?"

"For most of them. For one of them I have only Southern California. I may state that I also have a couple of manufacturers who have given me the states of Washington, Oregon and Nevada as well as California."

"I see," Mason said. "Do you have any manufacturers who have included the State of Arizona in your territory?"

"No, sir."

"Did you have?"

"Yes. I have had. I gave those contracts up because it was unprofitable to work an extra state where I didn't have enough contracts to make it economically profitable."

"You move around the state quite a bit then?"

"Yes."

"And up into Oregon and Washington?"

"Yes."

"If the Court please," Hamilton Burger objected, "I fail to see the object of this cross-examination. It appears to me that counsel is simply stalling for time, trying to put off—"

"That will do, Mr. District Attorney," Judge Alvord ruled. "In view of the very important testimony this witness has given on his direct examination, the Court is certainly going to permit defense counsel to have the widest latitude in the matter of cross-examination. I think these questions go to the background of the witness and I assume they will soon be directed as to the number of times the witness has seen Miss Barlow and for the purpose of determining whether there could have been any mistake."

Hamilton Burger smiled smugly. "Just let counsel ask this witness how many times he has seen Glamis Barlow and how well he knows her and the prosecution will have no objection, no objection whatever."

"I think that comment is uncalled for," Judge Alvord said. "The matter before the Court is an objection on your part and the objection is overruled. Proceed, Mr. Mason."

Mason said, "Where is your residence, Mr. Elliott? Where do you do your voting?"

"In Redding."

"In Redding!" Mason said.

"Yes, I have my office there. Much of my business is done by mail and I got started in the business in Redding. I am thinking of opening a Los Angeles office and—"

"Never mind what you are thinking," Hamilton Burger cautioned the witness. "Just answer Mr. Mason's questions and . . . I beg the Court's pardon. I will ask the Court to admonish the witness just to answer questions and not to volunteer information."

"Very well," Judge Alvord said. "I think the witness understands. Go on with your cross-examination, Mr. Mason."

Mason glanced at his watch, then back toward counsel table.

Della Street was making frantic signals to him.

"May I have just a moment, if the Court please?" Mason said.

"Very well, Mr. Mason. Please be brief, however."

Mason approached Della Street.

"Paul Drake gave me these," Della Street whispered. "Alan Hancock is now in the courtroom. He just arrived."

Della Street thrust some voluminous newspaper clippings and photographs into Mason's hands and whispered, her voice almost hysterical with excitement, "Take a look at Maureen Monroe's picture."

Mason looked at the photograph on top of the pile of papers, then, suddenly turning the photograph face down, approached the witness stand. For a moment he stood there contemplating the witness, his manner that of a man who is concentrating his every faculty.

"Please continue, Mr. Mason," Judge Alvord said.

Mason said, "Yes, Your Honor," then turned his piercing eyes on the witness. "So you live in Redding, Mr. Elliott?"

"Yes, sir."

"And the reason you opened your office in Redding was because you were living there at the time you went into the manufacturers' agency business?"

"Yes, sir."

"Just how did you get into the manufacturers' agency business, Mr. Elliott?"

"Oh, if the Court please, this certainly isn't legitimate cross-examination," Hamilton Burger said.

"I'm going to permit one or two more questions along these lines," Judge Alvord said. "I think defense counsel is, under the circumstances, entitled to get a foundation here."

"Answer the question," Mason said.

"Well, I returned from service in the army and was sort of at loose ends. I was living there in Redding and I—I noticed an ad by a manufacturer that wanted salesmen. I answered the ad and then I answered several more and started out in a small way selling merchandise just in Shasta County, and then I gradually branched out. I made good on the contracts and the manufacturers gave me more territory and I expanded my business."

"I see," Mason said. "Now, you had been in Redding before you went to the army and that is the reason you returned there?"

"Yes."

"What education have you had, Mr. Elliott?"

"I graduated from high school and had three years of college—"

"What high school?"

"Redding High School."

"While you were living in Redding," Mason asked, "did you know a family by the name of Monroe?"

There was a long period of silence.

"Can't you answer that question?" Mason asked.

"Are you referring to G. W. Monroe, the big lumber man?"

"Yes."

"I knew him, yes. I . . . yes, I knew him."

"And," Mason said, "did you know his daughter, Maureen Monroe?"

"Yes, I knew her."

Mason said, "Now, Mr. Elliott, you have testified that on the morning of the thirteenth you saw Glamis Barlow running from the workshop. I am going to show you this photograph and ask you if *this* isn't the person you saw running from the workshop."

"Just a moment, just a moment," Hamilton Burger said. "I want to see that photograph before it is shown to the witness."

The district attorney came bustling forward.

"Take a look," Mason said, handing him the photograph.

Hamilton Burger looked at the photograph, then

smiled. "No objection, Your Honor. No objection whatever."

Mason pushed the photograph in front of the witness. "Just answer the question," he said. "Isn't this a photograph of the person you saw running from the workshop? Didn't you see Maureen Monroe rather than Glamis Barlow?"

Had Mason hit the witness in the face with the photograph he could not have caused more consternation.

Hamilton Burger, watching the sagging jaw of the witness, jumped up, protesting and waving his hand as though to attract attention, but actually trying to reassure the witness. "Your Honor, Your Honor," he said, "the question is improper. The photograph is quite plainly that of Glamis Barlow and—"

"I suggest the district attorney be sworn," Mason said, "or perhaps he should look more closely. The caption which has been folded under the photograph states very plainly that it is a picture of Maureen Monroe, daughter of G. W. Monroe, whose engagement has just been announced to a wealthy young businessman of Arizona and New York."

Judge Alvord said, "Let me see that photograph, please."

Hamilton Burger came pushing toward the bench. "I think, Your Honor, there has been some trickery here, that this is another of Mr. Mason's attempts—"

"Let me see the photograph," Judge Alvord interrupted.

Mason handed up the photograph.

Judge Alvord studied the photograph, then turned down the sheet of flimsy which had been pasted on the photograph and folded under. He read the typewritten caption, then, without a word, handed the photograph back to Perry Mason and turned to the witness.

"Answer the question," Mason said, "and remember you're under oath. Was it Glamis Barlow or was it Maureen Monroe who ran out of that room?"

"Objection, Your Honor!" Hamilton Burger shouted. "We don't know that this photograph is properly authenticated. I object to the question on the ground that it is argumentative, that it calls for a conclusion of the witness, that it is not proper cross-examination, that no foundation has been laid."

"Overruled," Judge Alvord snapped. "The witness will answer the question."

"I—I—I don't know. Looking down from the window . . . now that I think of it . . . there is a very remarkable resemblance."

"I see," Mason said. "So *now* you are not prepared to swear that it *was* Glamis Barlow you saw running out of that workshop?"

"No, sir."

"You wish to change your testimony to state that you are not sure that it was Glamis Barlow you saw?"

"Yes, sir."

"Now, then," Mason said, "how long have you known Vera M. Martel?"

The witness began to fidget in the chair.

"You're under oath," Mason said. "How long have you known her?"

"Objected to as not proper cross-examination," Hamilton Burger said.

"Overruled," Judge Alvord snapped.

"I—I first met her about a month ago."

"Where?"

"In Las Vegas, Nevada."

"And how did you meet her?"

"I was introduced to her by a friend who told me that she was a very resourceful, daring private investigator."

"Now then," Mason said, leveling his finger at the witness, "did you or did you not enter into any business transaction with Vera Martel?"

The witness suddenly straightened. "I refuse to answer," he said.

Judge Alvord leaned forward ominously. "Upon what ground?"

The witness looked up defiantly. "Upon the ground," he said, "that the answer would tend to incriminate me."

Mason calmly walked back to the defense counsel table and sat down. "No further questions, Your Honor."

Hamilton Burger was on his feet. "Your Honor, this—this comes as a most complete surprise. A situation has developed here which certainly should be investigated. I want to find out more about that picture. I want to authenticate that picture. I feel that counsel has been guilty of a substitution here, that this picture of Glamis Barlow, has received a wrong caption and has been used deliberately to confuse this witness. I would like to ask for a continuance until I can verify this picture and ascertain what has happened."

"I have no objection to a continuance," Mason said. "The defense would like very much to have the district attorney verify the photograph, and I feel that the district attorney should pursue further the question of why this witness refuses to answer questions about his business deal with Vera Martel."

Judge Alvord said, "Mr. Mason, I am going to ask you if, to your knowledge, there has been any substitution of photographs or captions in this case."

"No, Your Honor. I have just received this photograph from a detective who arrived in this court just a few minutes ago in response to a telephone conversation with him I had last night in which I asked him to bring down photographs of Maureen Monroe."

In the silence that followed there was the sound of a woman sobbing.

Judge Alvord looked down at Nancy Gilman, who was crying.

"The Court is going to take a recess until tomorrow morning at ten o'clock," he said. And then, turning to Hamilton Burger, said, "I would suggest that, in the meantime, the police make every effort to get at the bottom of this. There is certainly a situation here which should be thoroughly investigated."

"Very well, Your Honor," a chastened Hamilton Burger said.

"Court's adjourned," Judge Alvord announced, and then gave Mason a long look of puzzled respect before arising and leaving the bench.

CHAPTER SEVENTEEN

IT WAS LATE that afternoon when Paul Drake entered Mason's office.

"Well," he said, "Hartley Elliott confessed. Of course, it all became apparent after Nancy Gilman made her statement.

"Nancy gave birth to twin girls. They were identical twins. She felt she couldn't keep them both, but she wanted one. Nancy was a remarkably intelligent, resourceful woman. She wanted to get a good home for the other daughter. She learned in some way that Mrs. G. W. Monroe of Redding had been confined and had given birth to a Mongoloid. The woman was heartbroken, so Nancy arranged a substitution and the Monroes returned to Redding with a beautiful daughter.

"The girls are absolutely identical. Even now it is almost impossible to tell them apart. When Hartley Elliott met Glamis he was so struck by the amazing resemblance that he started a quiet investigation. He wanted to find out about it, so he employed Vera Martel.

"It didn't take Vera long to run down what had happened. That was where Vera Martel tried the double-cross which turned out to be her death trap. Hartley Elliott thought they were either going to blackmail Nancy or sell information to Roger Calhoun.

"But Vera learned that John Yerman Hassell had left a sizable bequest in his will to whatever offspring Nancy might have during the six-month period following her affair with him. She learned that Nancy had very quietly convinced the Hassell heirs that Glamis was really the daughter of Hassell and had received a settlement. This is a tricky legal point. She didn't receive the inheritance; she received a settlement from the heirs.

"Also bear in mind that Maureen had never been formally adopted. The Monroes had simply palmed her off as their natural daughter.

"So Vera Martel began to wonder why it wouldn't be better to tell her accomplice she was working only on the blackmail angle but cut herself in on the real gravy by telling Maureen she thought there was some property Maureen didn't know about which Vera could recover. And so she paid Maureen ten thousand dollars for a half interest in all of this property.

"Maureen accepted the offer— Actually, her father, G. W. Monroe, didn't know anything about the transaction. He had come to Redding that night for an entirely different purpose.

"It wasn't until several days had passed that he learned what had happened from Maureen, then he told Maureen she was adopted.

"Suddenly Maureen found herself in an impossible situation. She was a foundling child who had been informally adopted into a wealthy family, but she was undoubtedly illegitimate. She knew that the Kimberlys would never consent to their socially prominent son marrying an illegitimate child, so Maureen started frantically hunting for Vera Martel.

"In order to find out just what Vera had in mind, Maureen trailed her. She trailed her to the Gilman residence where Vera had gone to have a showdown with Glamis. Glamis didn't know anything at all about what was happening, but Carter Gilman did know that Vera, a private detective, had been making inquiries about his wife and had been quietly trying to find out something about her background. So Gilman decided to consult you and telephoned for an appointment.

"Maureen followed Vera to the Gilman residence; Vera hurried back to the garage, walked through the darkroom and into the workshop where she was to meet her accomplice and arrange to bring Glamis and Nancy in for a showdown.

"Maureen followed Vera right into the room, accused Vera of being a crook, threw the ten thousand dollars in her face, then ran out of the workshop and around the house, jumped in her car and drove away. Later on she got a passkey somehow, went to Vera's Las Vegas office, let herself in and wrecked the place looking for the documentary evidence Vera had. She finally found it and then went to the casino and gambled for a while before she took a plane back to Redding.

"Hartley Elliott was meeting Vera in the garage. The run-down battery was all part of the plan. He gave her the result of what information he had been able to acquire and was to give her more last-minute instructions. When he heard Maureen coming he hid in the shadows of the darkroom. After Maureen had left, Hartley, of course, realized that Vera had sold him out. Regardless of the fact Maureen had tried to return the ten thousand, Vera Martel had her signature on a document of assignment. Elliott became enraged at the double-cross and started choking Vera. He says in his confession he never intended to kill her but only to discipline her and make her afraid of him, and that probably is true. However, he did choke her to death. When he saw she was dead he crammed her body into the trunk of Gilman's automobile. Then he saw Gilman coming out of the house, so Elliott slipped into the darkroom and hid. Then, when Gilman passed through the darkroom and entered the workshop, Elliott dashed out of the darkroom, down the driveway, back in the front door and up to his room. Naturally, he had no opportunity to pick up the money that had been flung all over the floor of the workroom."

Della Street said, "So Gilman must have seen Vera Martel as she entered the garage."

"That's right," Drake said. "He was eating breakfast and reading the paper. He looked up just as Vera Martel went into the darkroom. That bothered him. Then, later on, he saw Maureen running out of the workshop and, of course, he thought it was Glamis.

"Gilman wanted to go out and investigate but he had to get rid of Muriell, so he asked her to cook some food which he didn't really want. Muriell, however, knowing he had eaten enough, stalled around, hoping he would countermand the order.

"Gilman finally got out to the workshop, found the money all over the floor and the signs of struggle. He jumped in his car, drove around looking for Vera. He found where her car was parked but he couldn't find her. It never occurred to him that her body was actually in the trunk of his car. When he couldn't find Vera he drove his car to the place where he usually caught the bus, parked it and took the bus to town.

"Hartley Elliott had Vera's car keys and her purse. He first wanted to move Vera's car, then he could hardly believe his good luck when he found Gilman's car parked at the bus stop.

"He short-circuited the switch, started the car, drove to the mountain road, concealed Vera's body, then returned Gilman's car to the place where it had been parked, got in Vera's car, drove up to where he had left the body, put Vera's body in the car, drove the car over the cliff, hitchhiked back and went about his business. He felt certain that when the body was found it would either be considered accidental death or, if it was considered homicide, Carter Gilman would be the one who took the rap.

"In the meantime, Elliott now had information that would enable him to blackmail several people but he didn't dare make a move until the hue and cry over Vera's death had died down."

"How did they get a confession out of Elliott?" Mason asked.

"You can thank Lieutenant Tragg for that," Drake said. "Tragg began to put two and two together and that stay in the tank on the contempt charge had really taken the starch out of Elliott. He caved in once they began to pour the questions at him."

"And Maureen?" Della Street asked sympathetically.

"Apparently," Drake said, "the Kimberlys are real people. According to latest reports, Harvey Kimberly is standing by Maureen and the family is standing by both of them. The wedding is going ahead as planned."

Perry Mason took a long breath. "Well," he said, "it just goes to show that a lawyer should always keep fighting."

Della Street looked at him with an admiration that was almost worshipful. "Did you," she asked, "have any idea of this?"

"I began to consider it a definite possibility," Mason said, "when I kept thinking about the peculiar chart run by Nancy Gilman when she took that lie-detector test and was asked about *a* daughter.

"There could be no question that Glamis Barlow was her daughter and yet, when she answered the question that she had had *a* daughter, the chart showed an emotional disturbance indicating she was lying.

"But I confess it wasn't until after I had finished talking with Alan Hancock on the phone that the definite possibilities of the situation began to dawn on me. Even at that, I had to stake everything on a gamble."

"That took nerve," Drake said admiringly.

Mason shook his head. "There was only one way to go," he said. "If I had stopped I'd have been engulfed, and if I'd gone any other way I'd have fallen over a precipice. . . . In fact, that's the only technique to use . . . when you get in a fight, *keep moving*."